BURT'S WAY HOME

THANK YOU:
ANNIE KOYAMA, ED KANERVA, HELEN KOYAMA, LINDSAY ARCHIBALD, AARON COSTAIN,
JEN BREACH, NASEEM HRAB, KATE BEATON, MOM & DAD

TEXT AND ILLUSTRATIONS COPYRIGHT © 2016 BY JOHN MARTZ

TUNDRA BOOKS, AN IMPRINT OF PENGUIN RANDOM HOUSE CANADA YOUNG READERS,
A DIVISION OF PENGUIN RANDOM HOUSE OF CANADA LIMITED

PUBLISHED BY TUNDRA BOOKS, 2022
FIRST PUBLISHED BY KOYAMA PRESS, 2016

LIBRARY AND ARCHIVES CANADA CATALOGUING IN PUBLICATION

TITLE: BURT'S WAY HOME / JOHN MARTZ.
NAMES: MARTZ, JOHN, 1978- AUTHOR, ILLUSTRATOR.
DESCRIPTION: PREVIOUSLY PUBLISHED: TORONTO, ONTARIO: KOYAMA PRESS, 2016.
IDENTIFIERS: CANADIANA (PRINT) 2021021743X | CANADIANA (EBOOK) 20210217448 |
ISBN 9780735271029 (HARDCOVER) | ISBN 9780735271036 (EPUB)
SUBJECTS: LCGFT: GRAPHIC NOVELS.
CLASSIFICATION: LCC PN6733.M37 B87 2022 | DDC J741.5/971—DC23

PUBLISHED SIMULTANEOUSLY IN THE UNITED STATES OF AMERICA BY TUNDRA BOOKS OF
NORTHERN NEW YORK, AN IMPRINT OF PENGUIN RANDOM HOUSE CANADA YOUNG READERS,
A DIVISION OF PENGUIN RANDOM HOUSE OF CANADA LIMITED

LIBRARY OF CONGRESS CONTROL NUMBER: 2021938699

DESIGNED BY JOHN MARTZ
THE ARTWORK IN THIS BOOK WAS CREATED DIGITALLY.
THE TEXT WAS SET IN BULLETIN TYPEWRITER AND ORIGIN STORY,
A TYPEFACE CREATED FOR THIS BOOK.

PRINTED IN CHINA

WWW.PENGUINRANDOMHOUSE.CA

1   2   3   4   5   26   25   24   23   22

Penguin
Random House
tundra   TUNDRA BOOKS

BURT'S WAY HOME

John Martz

tundra

Burt and I live at
the edge of town, in
the small apartment
building at the bottom
of Mount Maple.

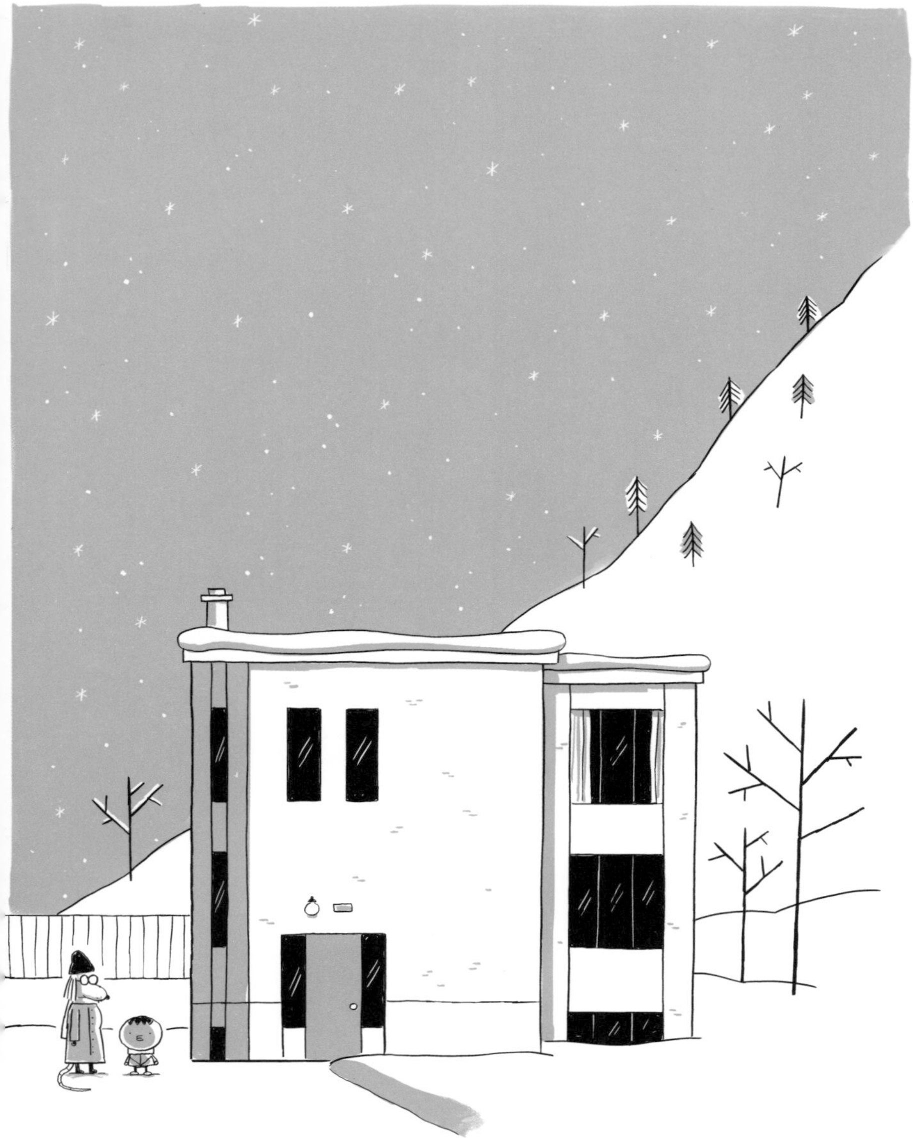

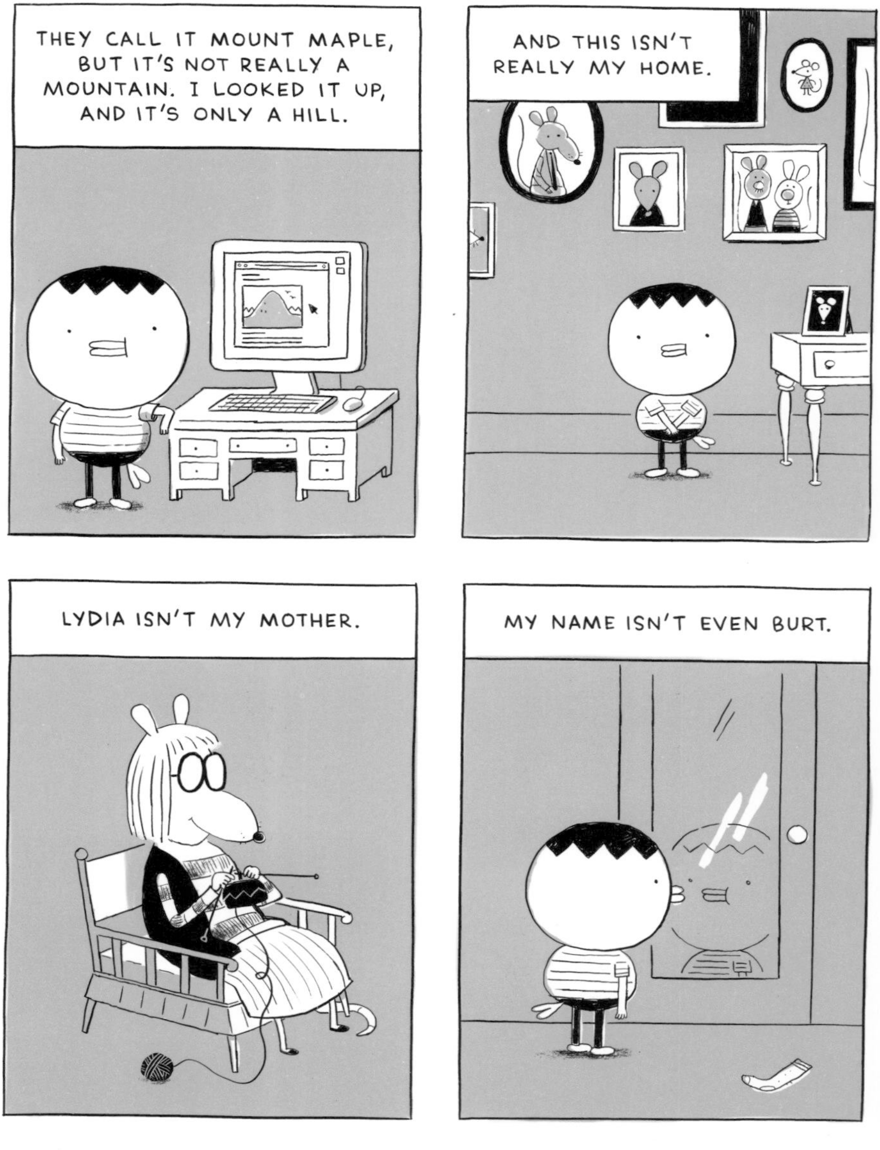
THEY CALL IT MOUNT MAPLE, BUT IT'S NOT REALLY A MOUNTAIN. I LOOKED IT UP, AND IT'S ONLY A HILL.
AND THIS ISN'T REALLY MY HOME.
LYDIA ISN'T MY MOTHER.
MY NAME ISN'T EVEN BURT.

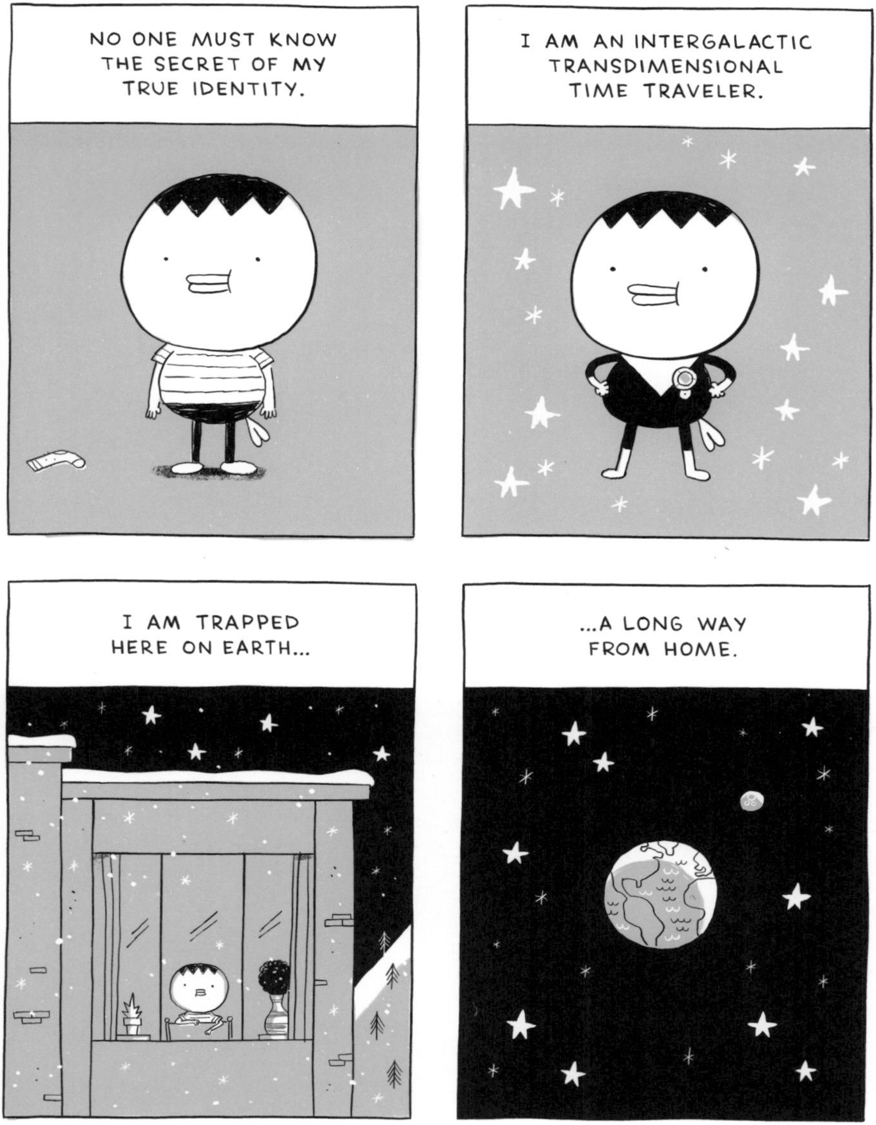
NO ONE MUST KNOW THE SECRET OF MY TRUE IDENTITY.
I AM AN INTERGALACTIC TRANSDIMENSIONAL TIME TRAVELER.
I AM TRAPPED HERE ON EARTH...
...A LONG WAY FROM HOME.

I hope he's happy here.

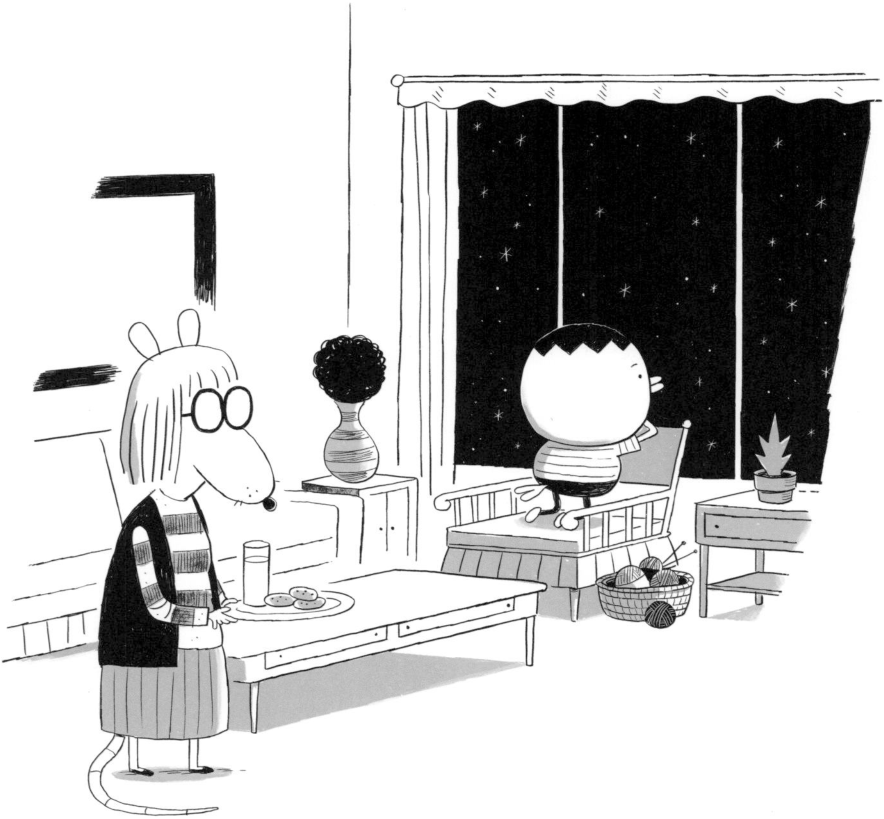

MY PARENTS ARE INTERGALACTIC TRANSDIMENSIONAL TIME TRAVELERS TOO.

WE ARE EXPLORERS AND OBSERVERS FROM THE PLANET MOD IN THE KUBERP SYSTEM.

OUR ADVANCED TECHNOLOGY ALLOWS US TO TRAVEL INSTANTLY THROUGH TIME AND SPACE.

THIS DEVICE IS CALLED THE CHRONOMORPHIC ENGINE.

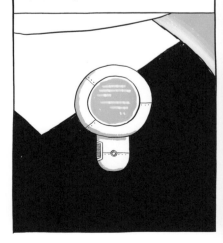

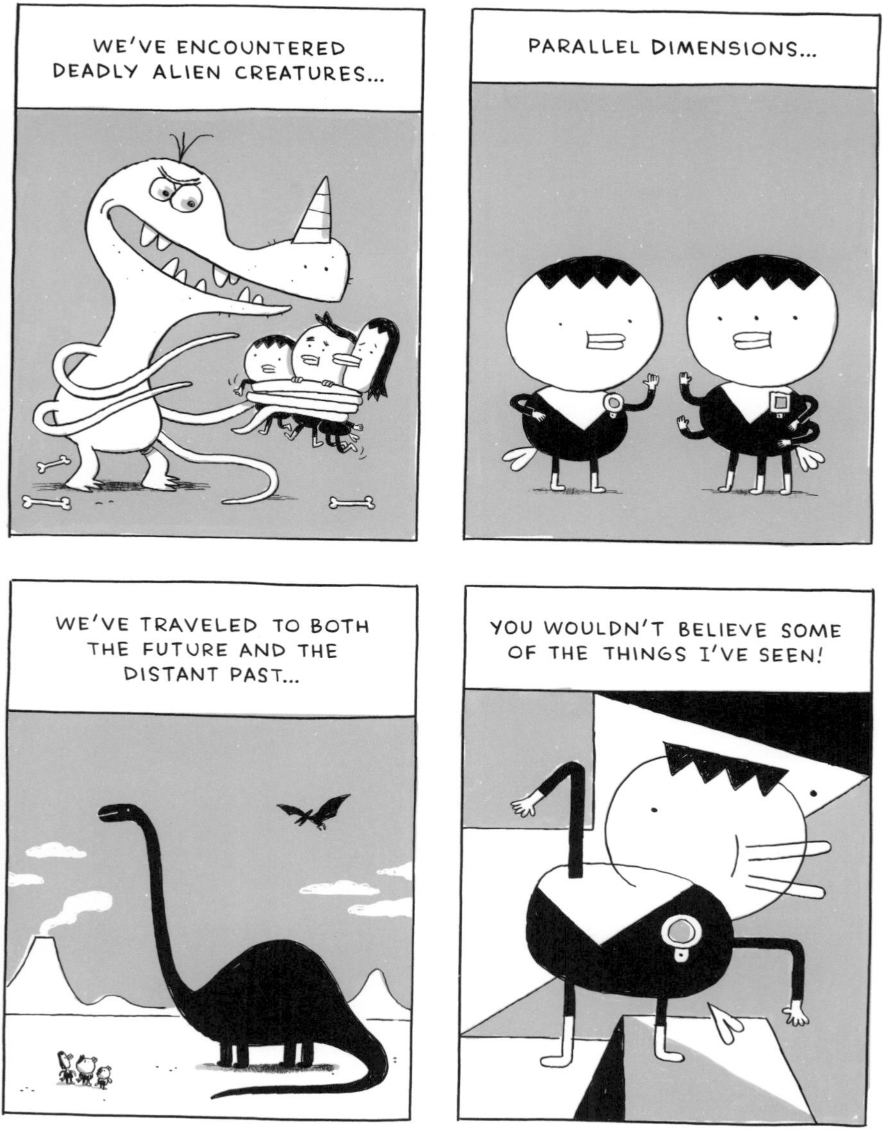
WE'VE ENCOUNTERED DEADLY ALIEN CREATURES...
PARALLEL DIMENSIONS...
WE'VE TRAVELED TO BOTH THE FUTURE AND THE DISTANT PAST...
YOU WOULDN'T BELIEVE SOME OF THE THINGS I'VE SEEN!

I can't even begin to imagine what he's been through.

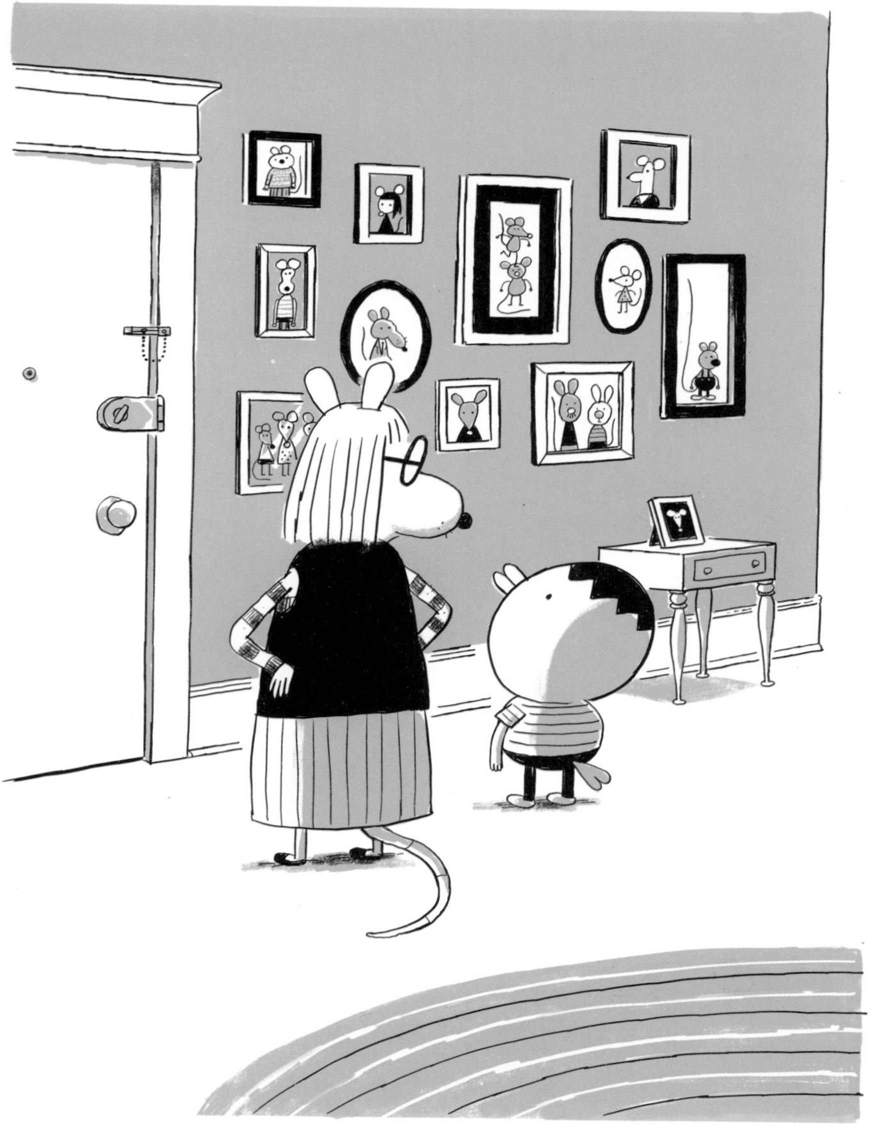

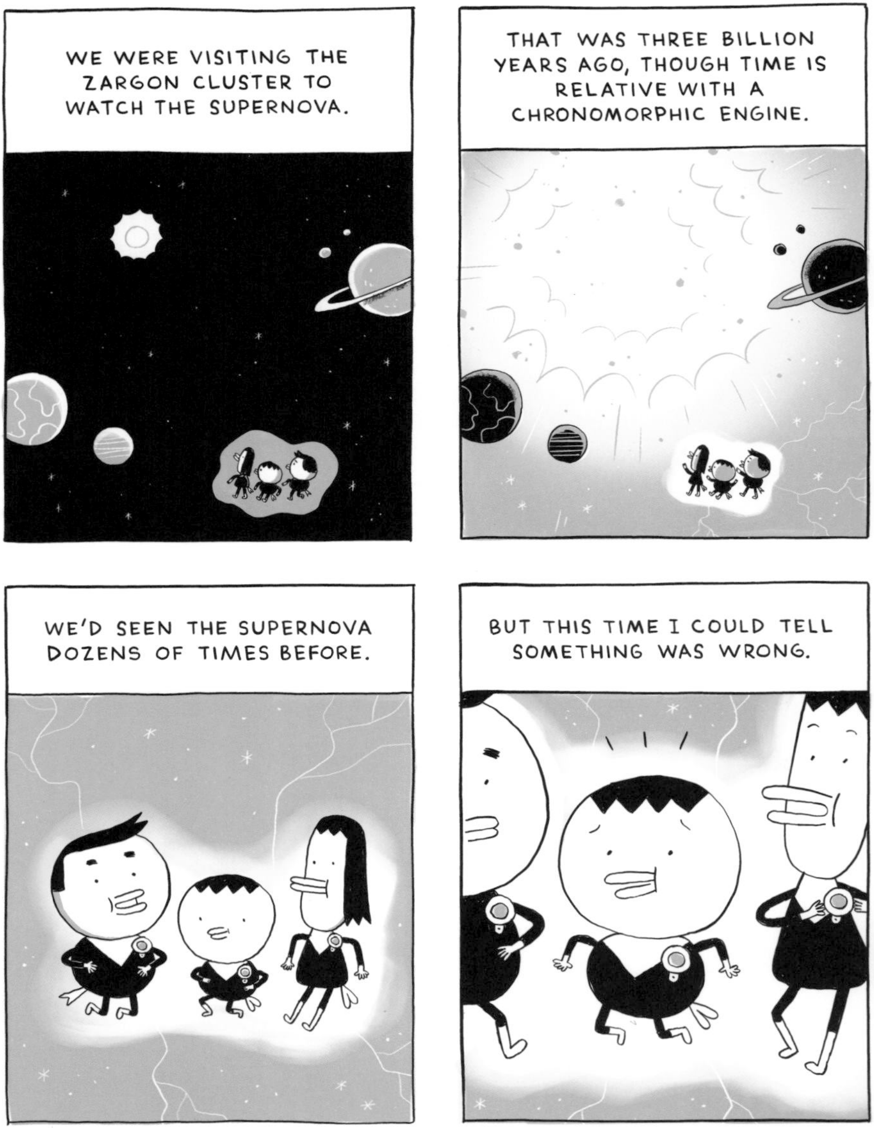
WE WERE VISITING THE ZARGON CLUSTER TO WATCH THE SUPERNOVA.
THAT WAS THREE BILLION YEARS AGO, THOUGH TIME IS RELATIVE WITH A CHRONOMORPHIC ENGINE.
WE'D SEEN THE SUPERNOVA DOZENS OF TIMES BEFORE.
BUT THIS TIME I COULD TELL SOMETHING WAS WRONG.

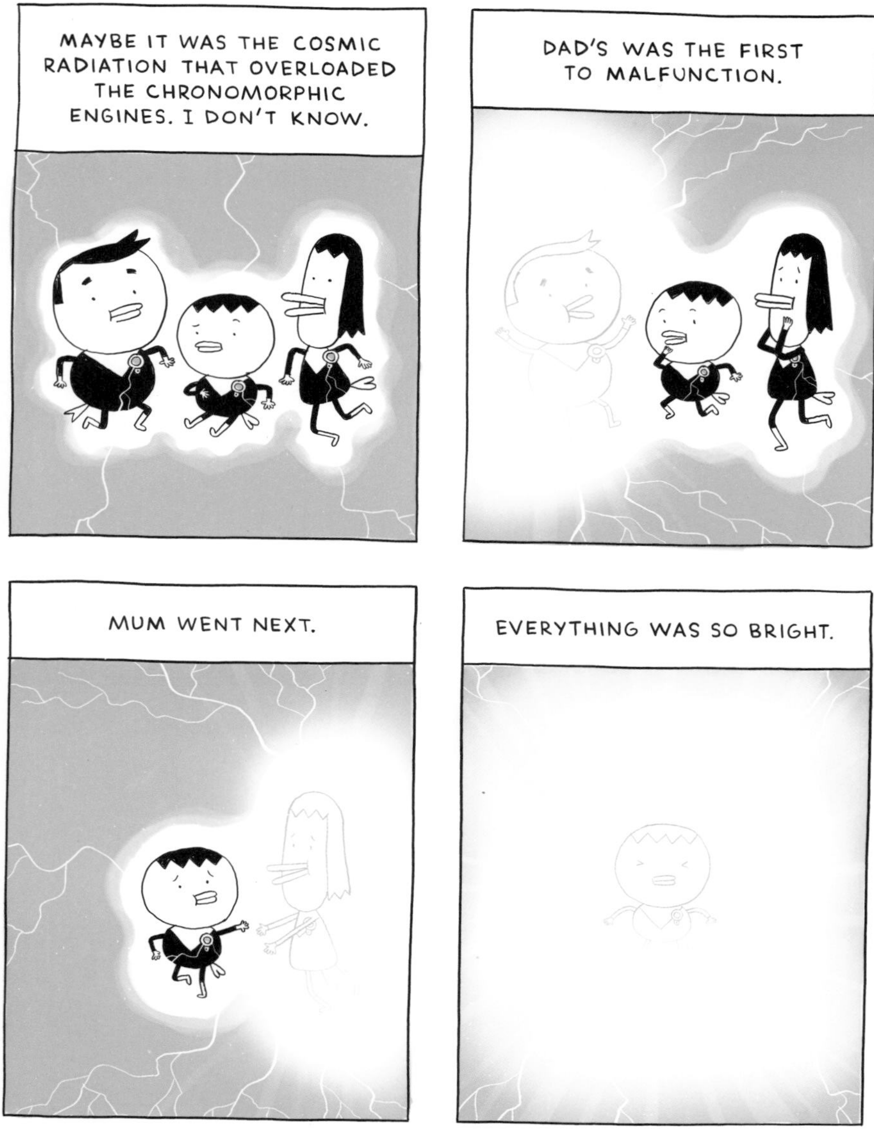
MAYBE IT WAS THE COSMIC RADIATION THAT OVERLOADED THE CHRONOMORPHIC ENGINES. I DON'T KNOW.
DAD'S WAS THE FIRST TO MALFUNCTION.
MUM WENT NEXT.
EVERYTHING WAS SO BRIGHT.

I know it will take
some time before he
settles in.

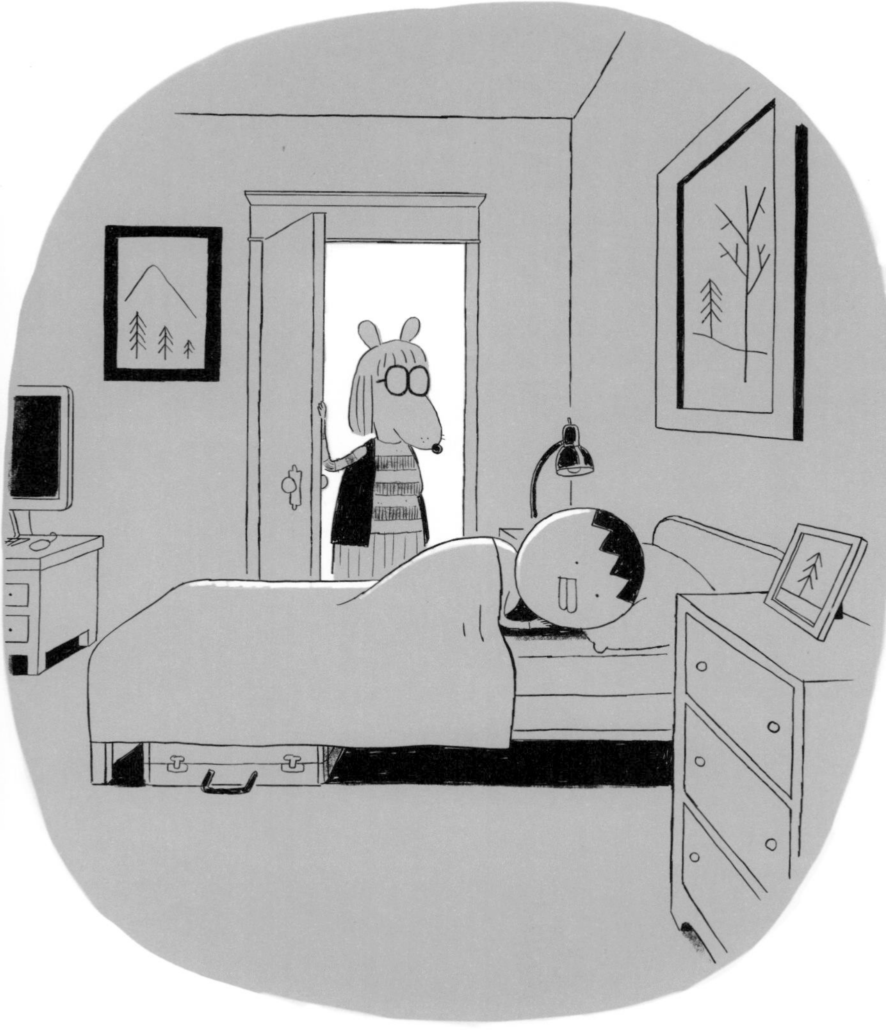

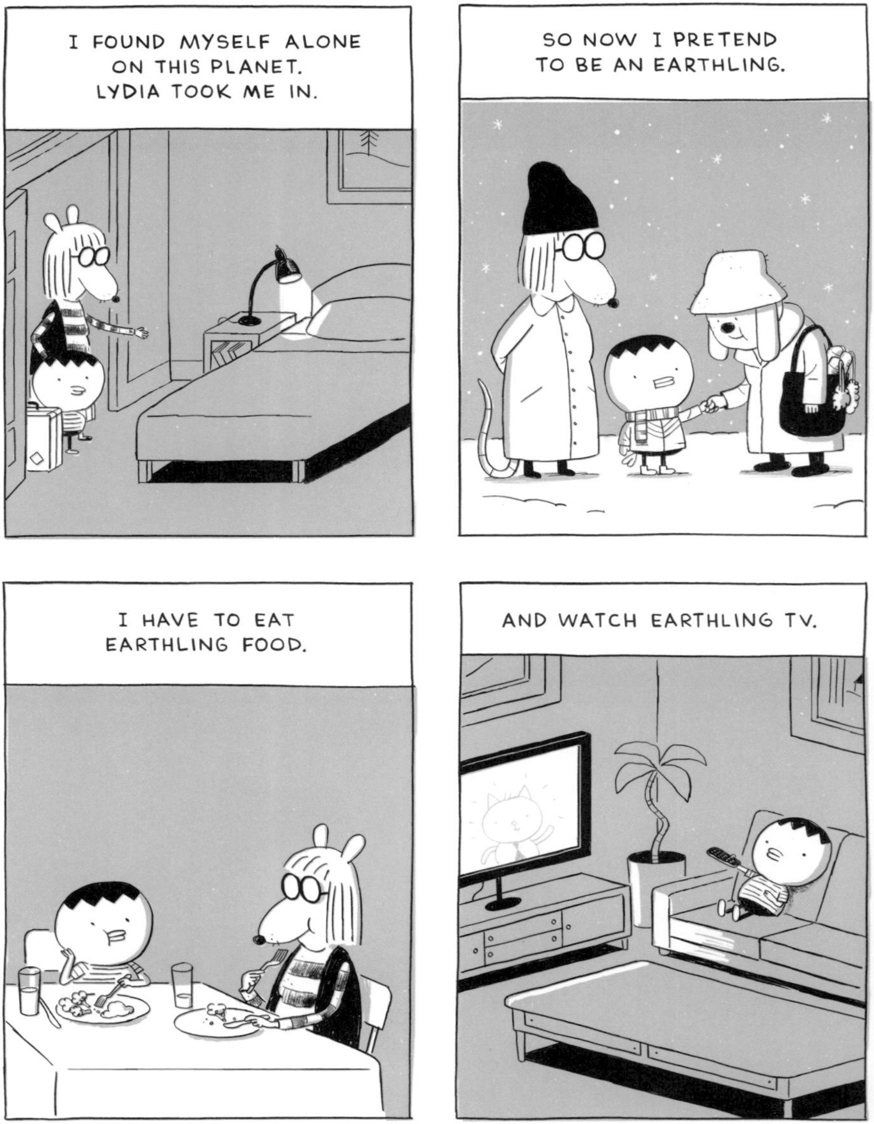
I FOUND MYSELF ALONE ON THIS PLANET. LYDIA TOOK ME IN.
SO NOW I PRETEND TO BE AN EARTHLING.
I HAVE TO EAT EARTHLING FOOD.
AND WATCH EARTHLING TV.

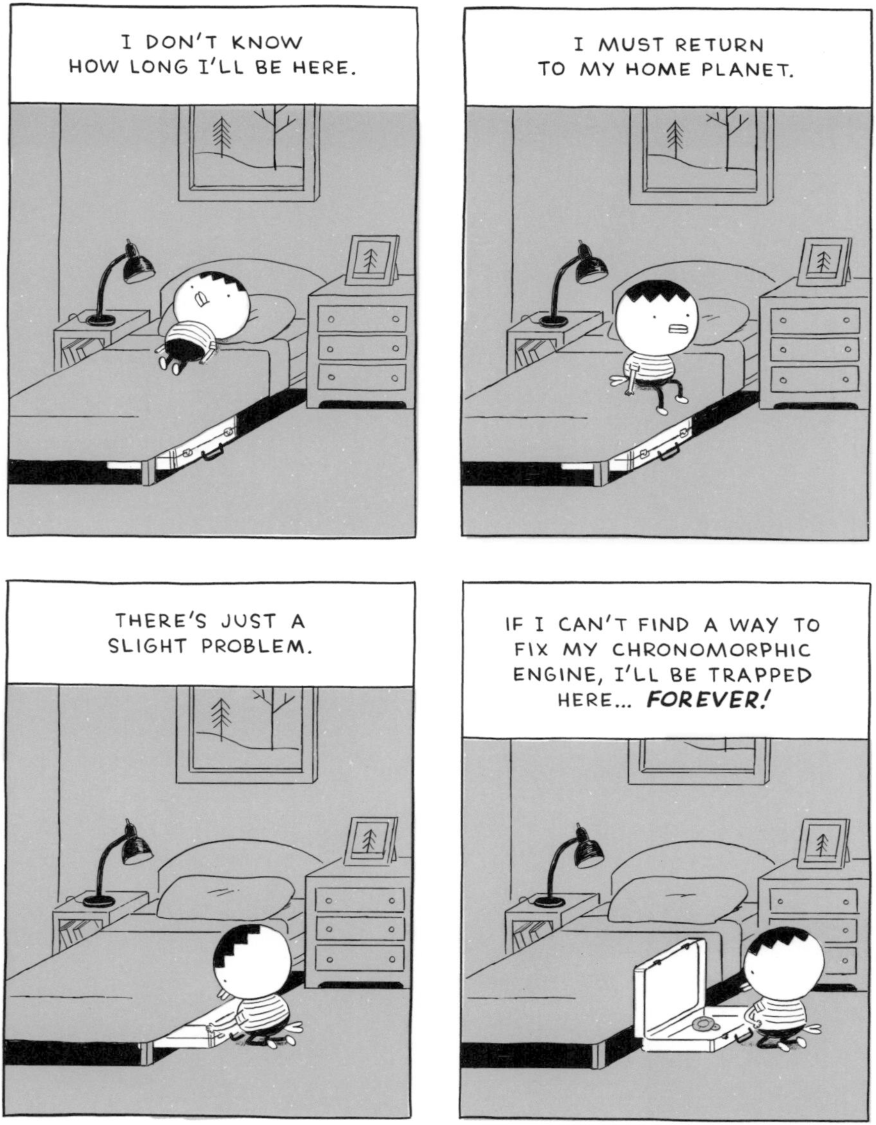
I DON'T KNOW HOW LONG I'LL BE HERE.
I MUST RETURN TO MY HOME PLANET.
THERE'S JUST A SLIGHT PROBLEM.
IF I CAN'T FIND A WAY TO FIX MY CHRONOMORPHIC ENGINE, I'LL BE TRAPPED HERE... *FOREVER!*

Things have begun to
go missing around the
apartment.

I spent hours today
looking for the TV
remote.

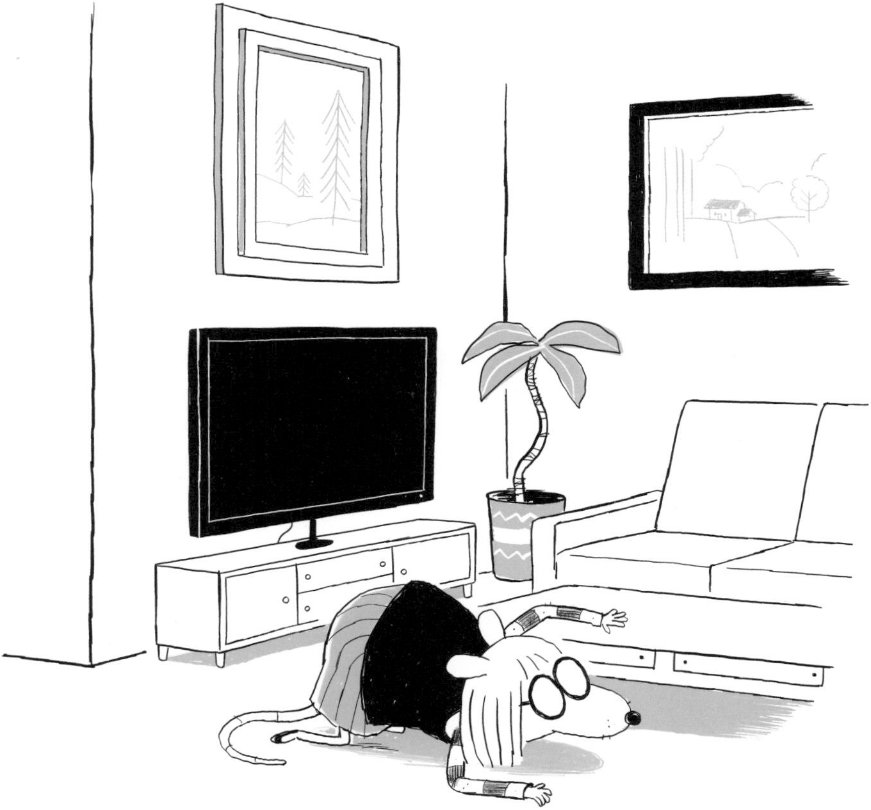

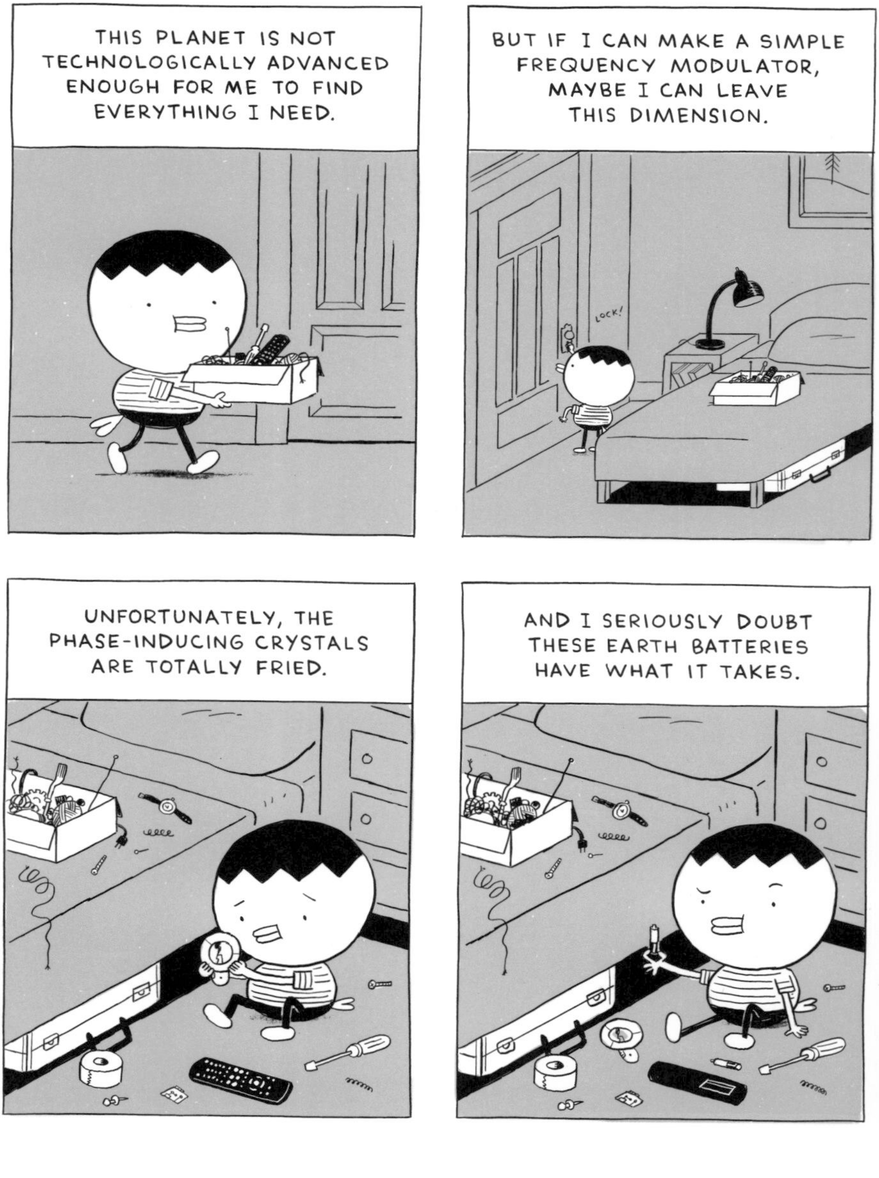
THIS PLANET IS NOT TECHNOLOGICALLY ADVANCED ENOUGH FOR ME TO FIND EVERYTHING I NEED.
BUT IF I CAN MAKE A SIMPLE FREQUENCY MODULATOR, MAYBE I CAN LEAVE THIS DIMENSION.
LOCK!
UNFORTUNATELY, THE PHASE-INDUCING CRYSTALS ARE TOTALLY FRIED.
AND I SERIOUSLY DOUBT THESE EARTH BATTERIES HAVE WHAT IT TAKES.

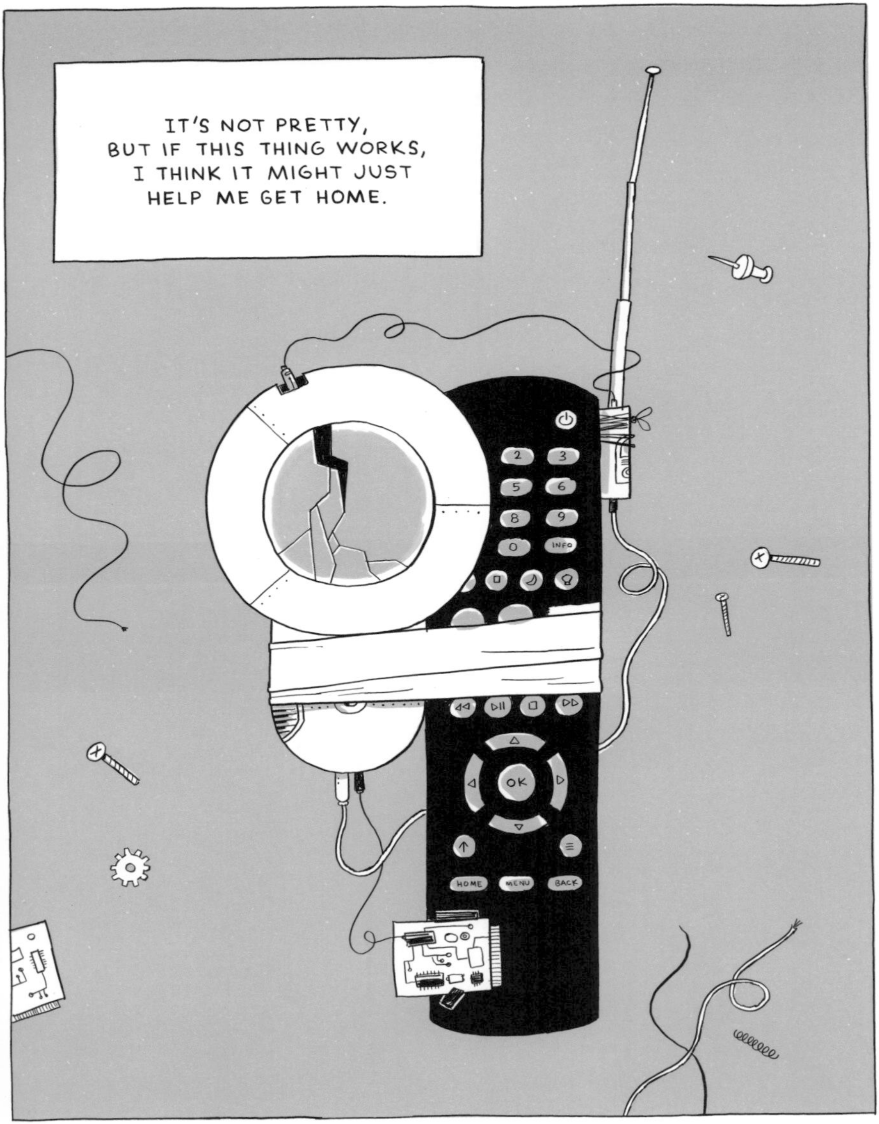
IT'S NOT PRETTY, BUT IF THIS THING WORKS, I THINK IT MIGHT JUST HELP ME GET HOME.

I guess it's supposed to be some sort of radio or something.

I only wish he would wear a hat.

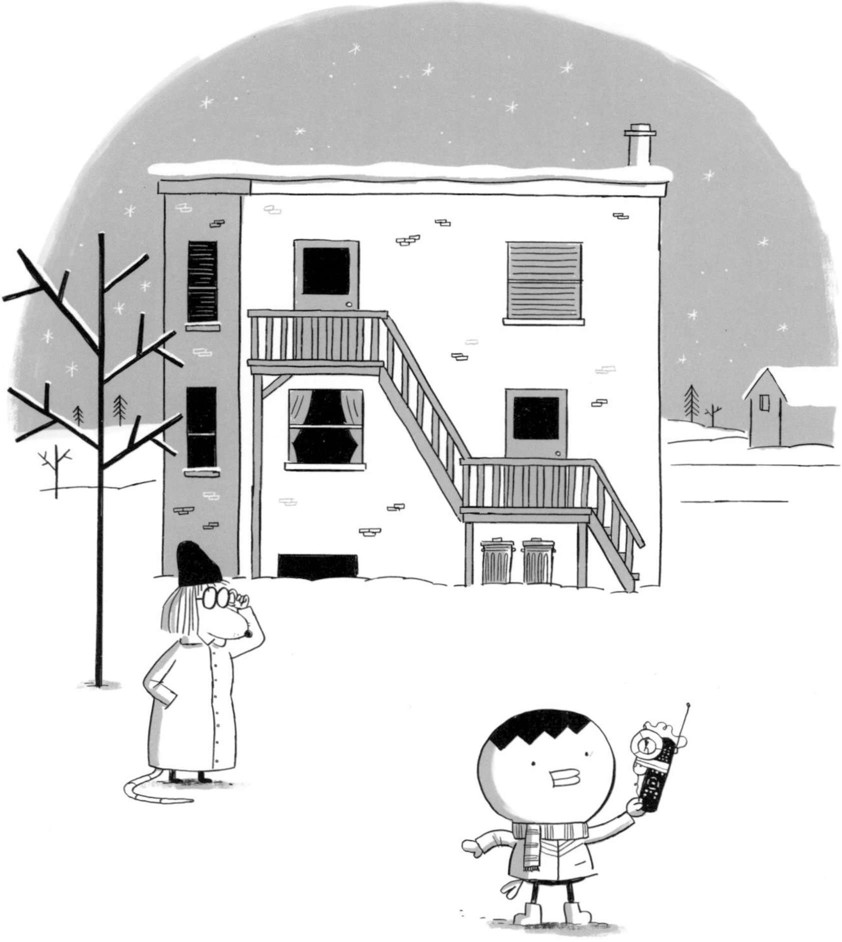

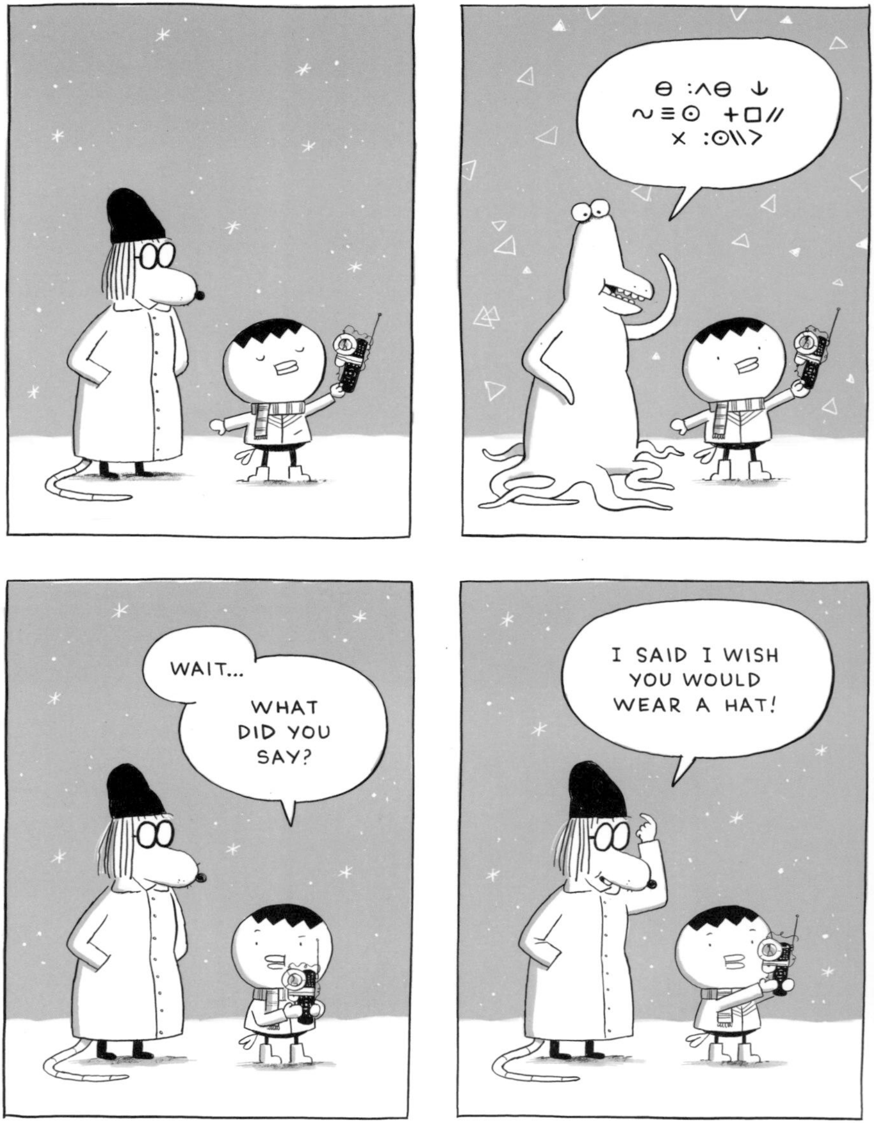
WAIT...
WHAT DID YOU SAY?
I SAID I WISH YOU WOULD WEAR A HAT!

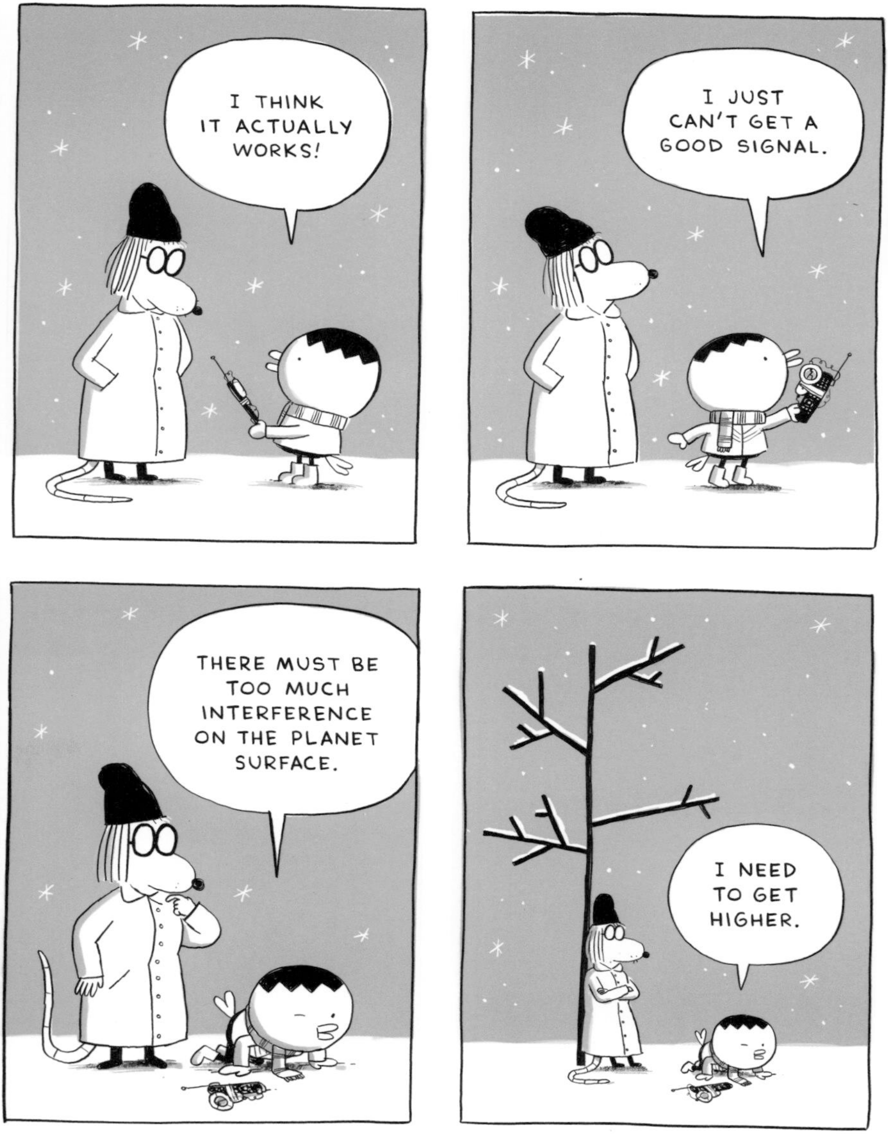
I THINK IT ACTUALLY WORKS!
I JUST CAN'T GET A GOOD SIGNAL.
THERE MUST BE TOO MUCH INTERFERENCE ON THE PLANET SURFACE.
I NEED TO GET HIGHER.

When neighbors ask,
I tell them he's
conducting a science
experiment for school.

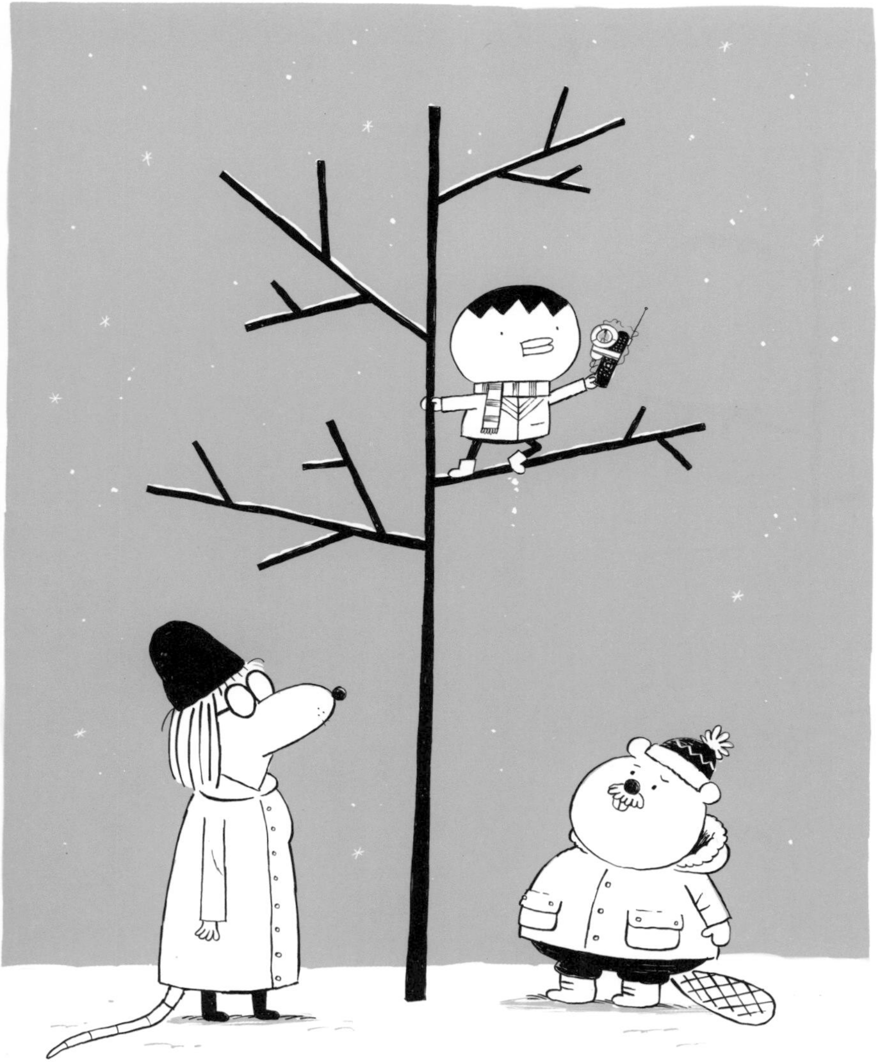

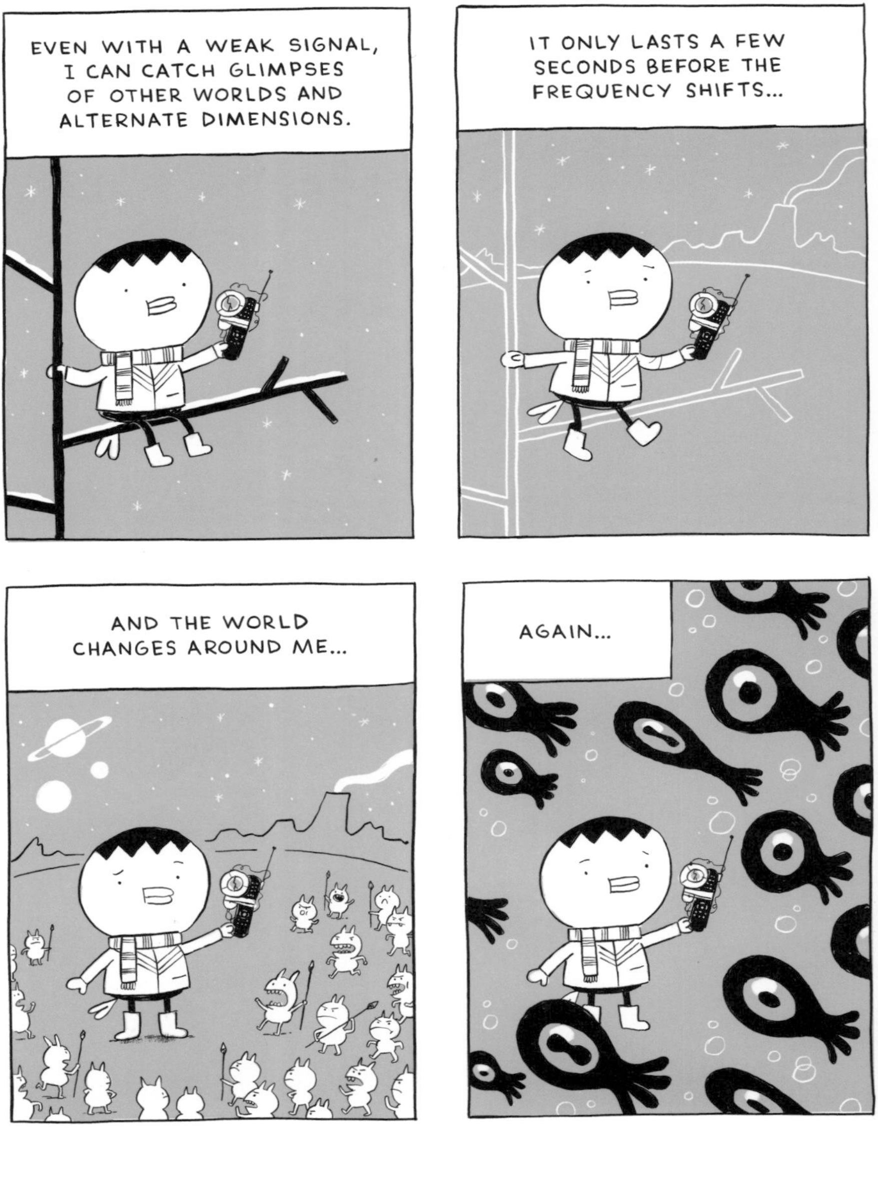
EVEN WITH A WEAK SIGNAL, I CAN CATCH GLIMPSES OF OTHER WORLDS AND ALTERNATE DIMENSIONS.
IT ONLY LASTS A FEW SECONDS BEFORE THE FREQUENCY SHIFTS...
AND THE WORLD CHANGES AROUND ME...
AGAIN...

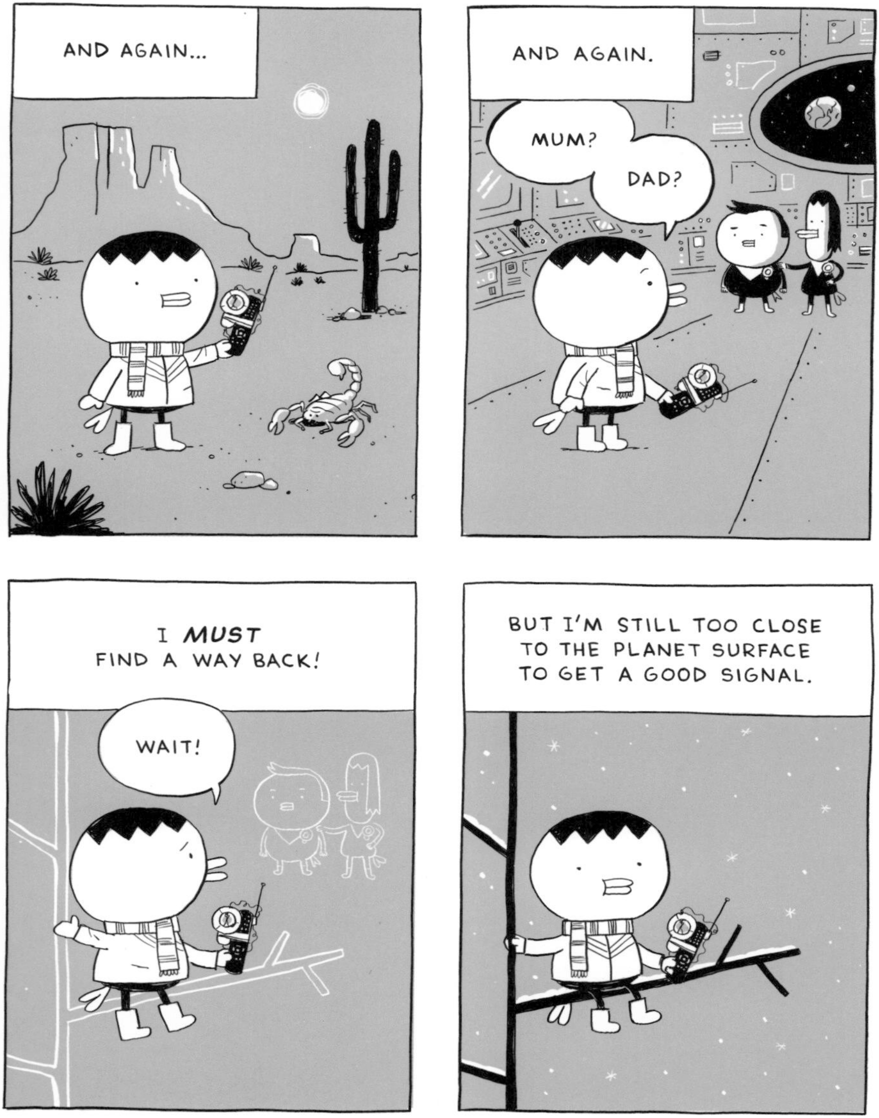
AND AGAIN...
AND AGAIN.
MUM?
DAD?
I MUST FIND A WAY BACK!
WAIT!
BUT I'M STILL TOO CLOSE TO THE PLANET SURFACE TO GET A GOOD SIGNAL.

He's been running around up there for hours.

He must be freezing.

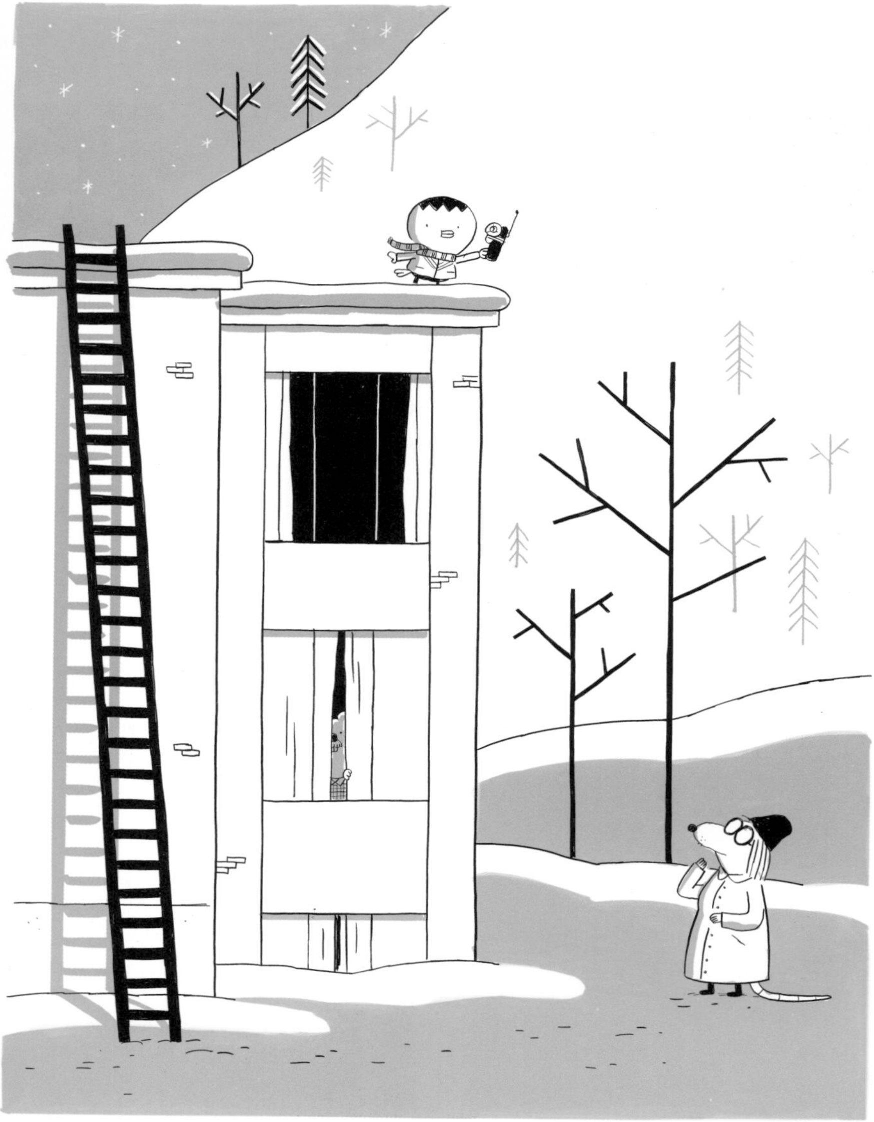

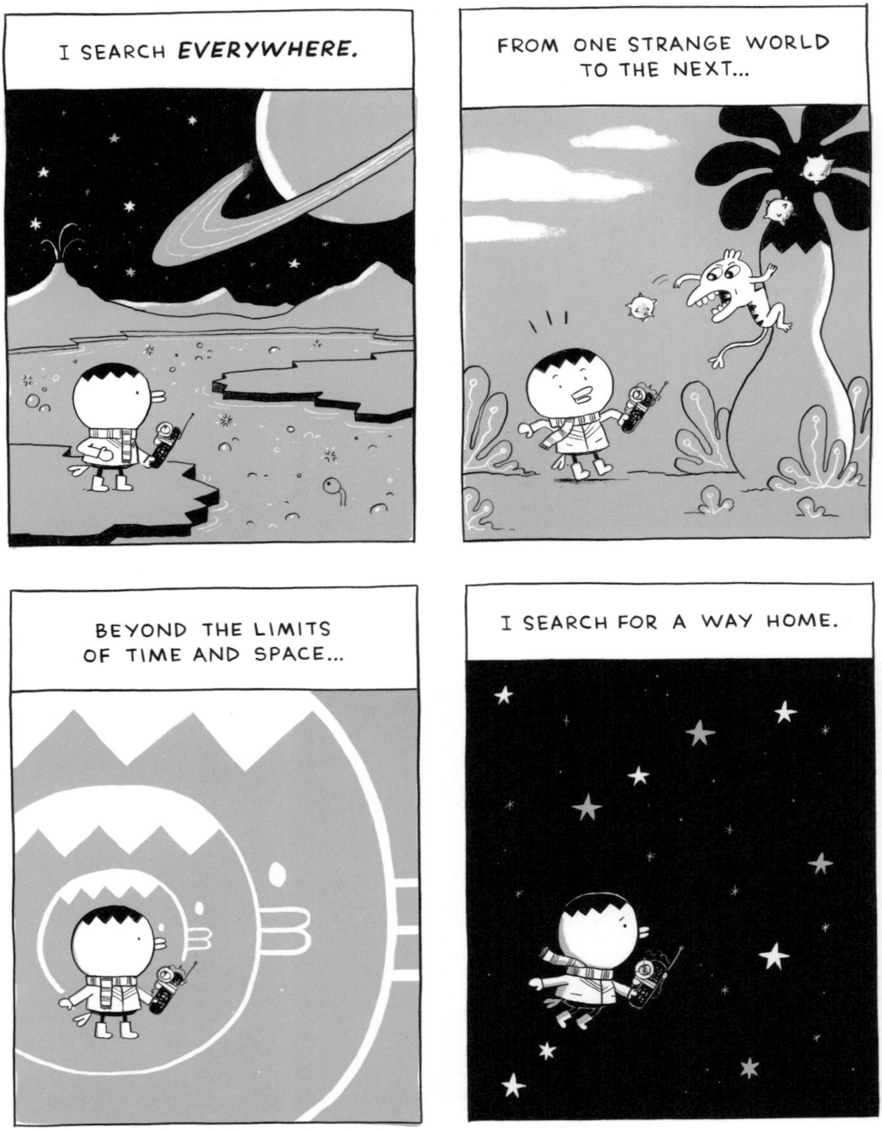
I SEARCH **EVERYWHERE.**
FROM ONE STRANGE WORLD TO THE NEXT...
BEYOND THE LIMITS OF TIME AND SPACE...
I SEARCH FOR A WAY HOME.

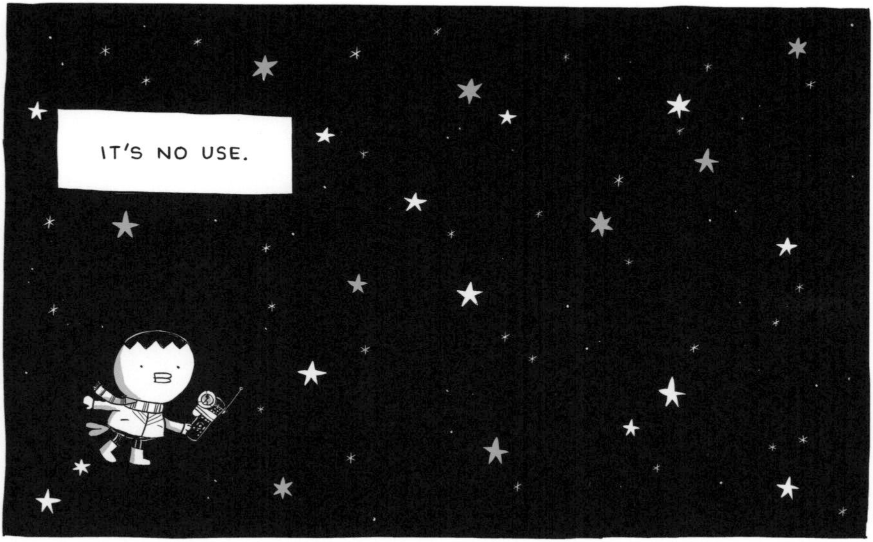
IT'S NO USE.

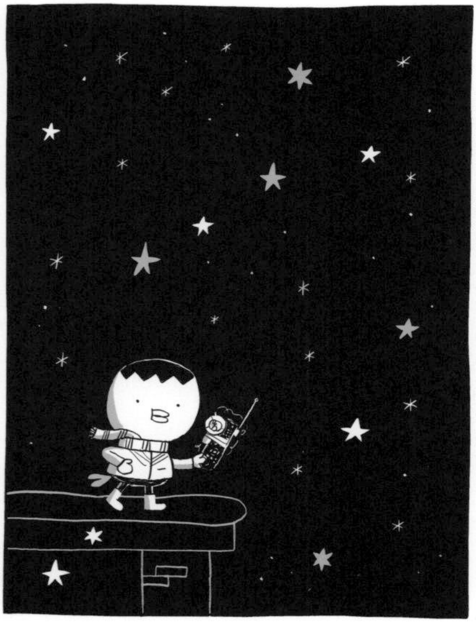

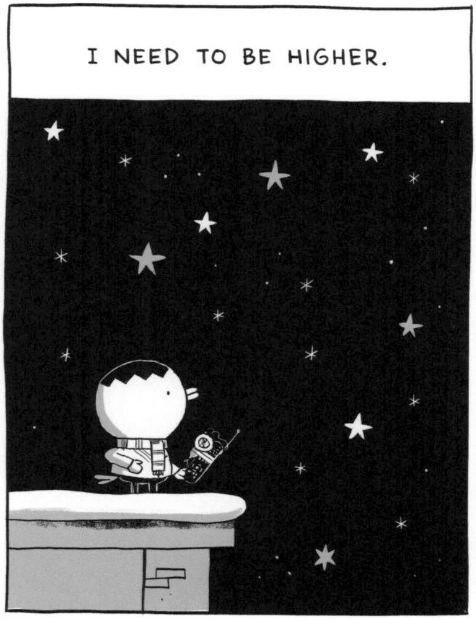
I NEED TO BE HIGHER.

It's been quite a day.
No wonder Burt went
straight to bed.

It's getting late and
I should probably get
some sleep too.

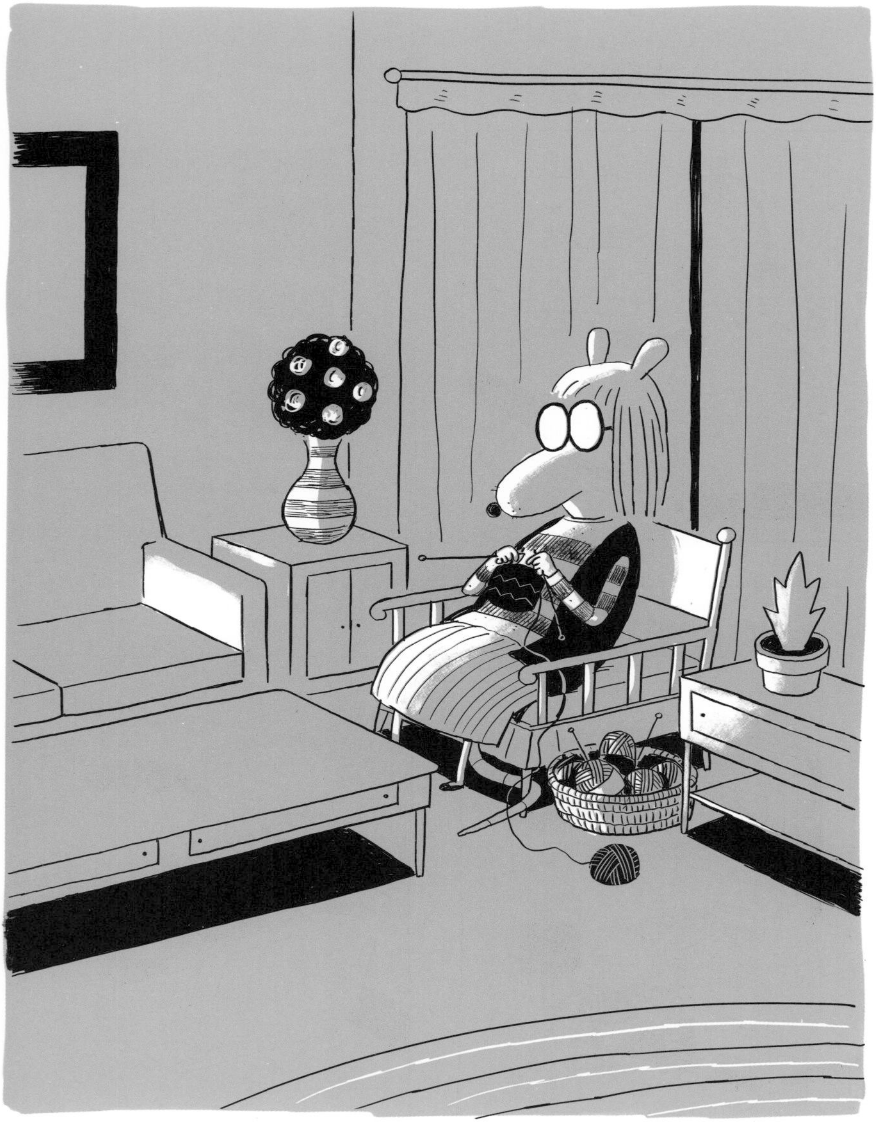

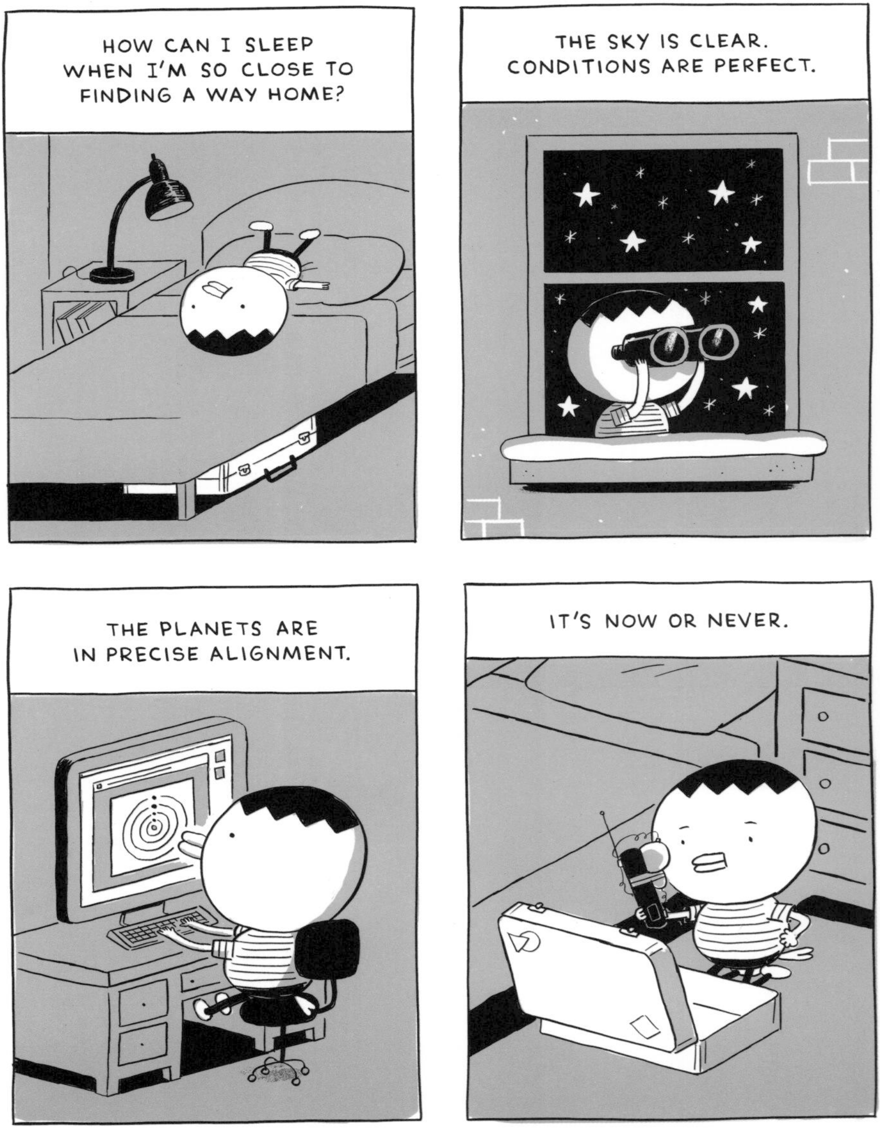
HOW CAN I SLEEP WHEN I'M SO CLOSE TO FINDING A WAY HOME?
THE SKY IS CLEAR. CONDITIONS ARE PERFECT.
THE PLANETS ARE IN PRECISE ALIGNMENT.
IT'S NOW OR NEVER.

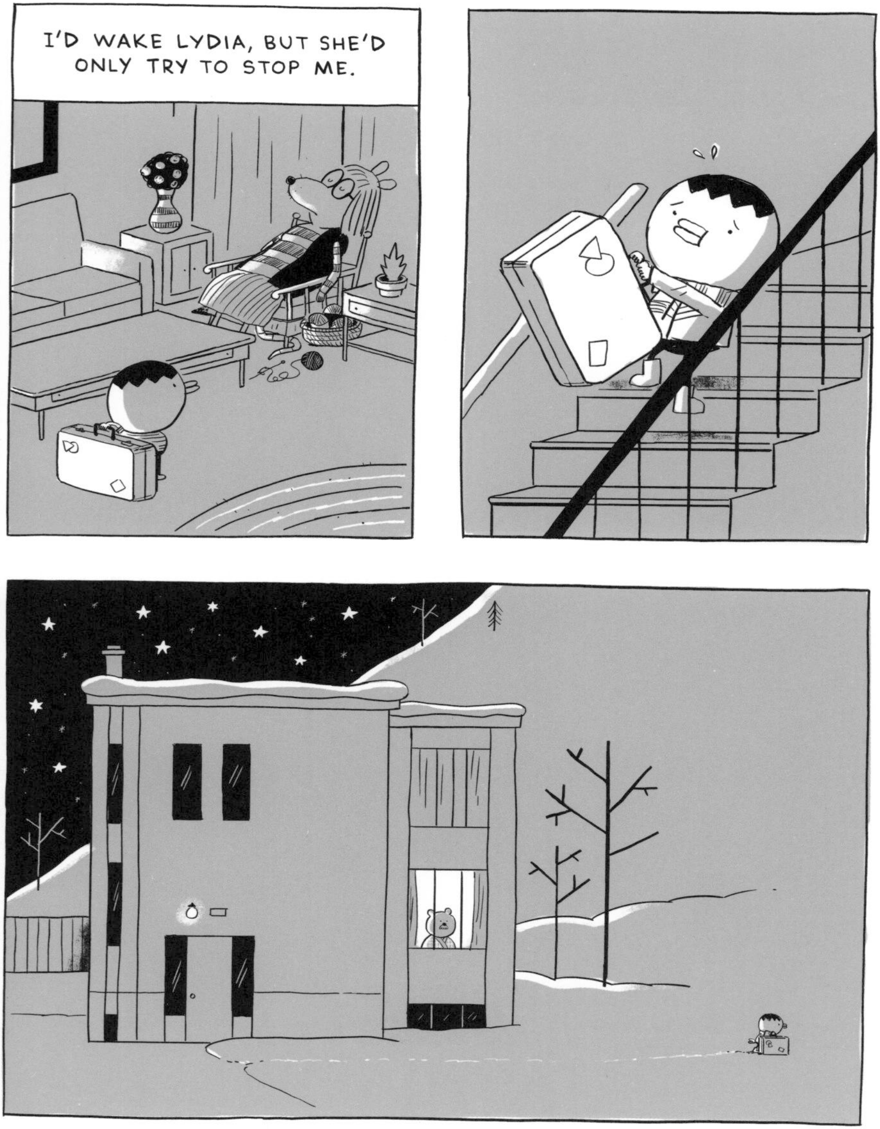
I'D WAKE LYDIA, BUT SHE'D ONLY TRY TO STOP ME.

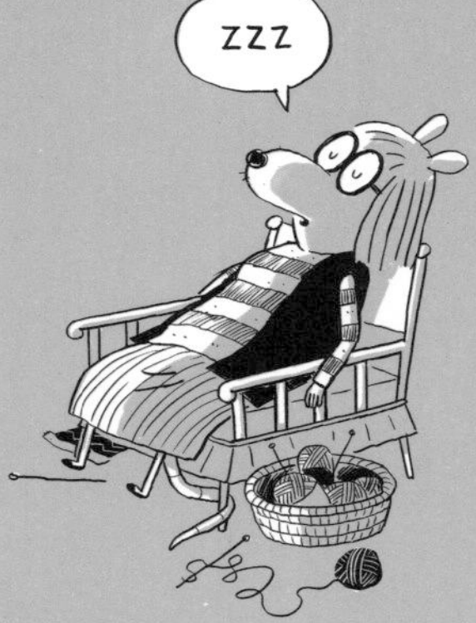
ZZZ

Knock! Knock! Knock!

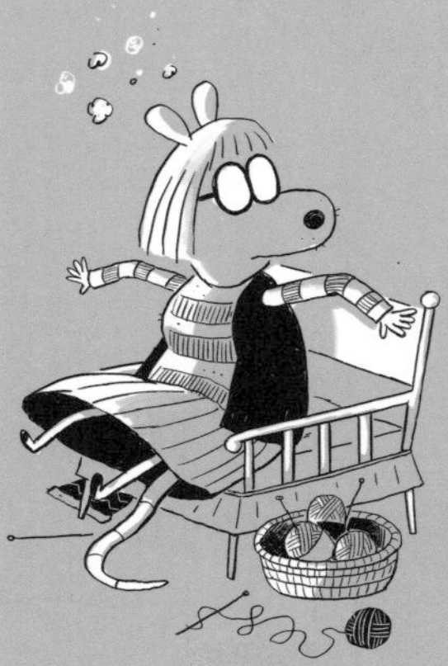

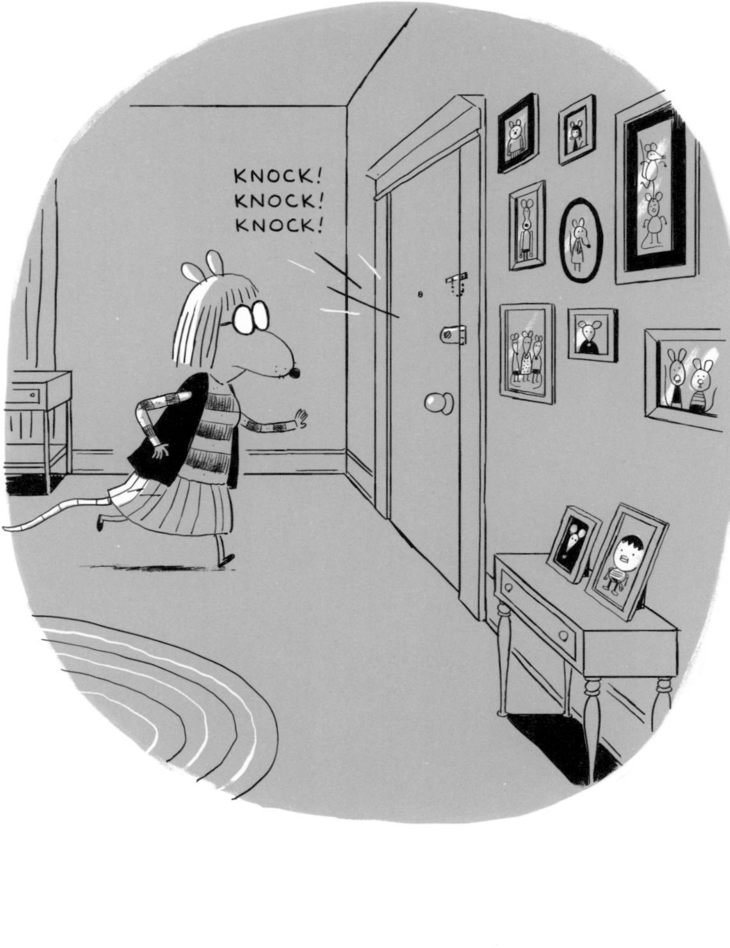
KNOCK!
KNOCK!
KNOCK!

What is Burt thinking?

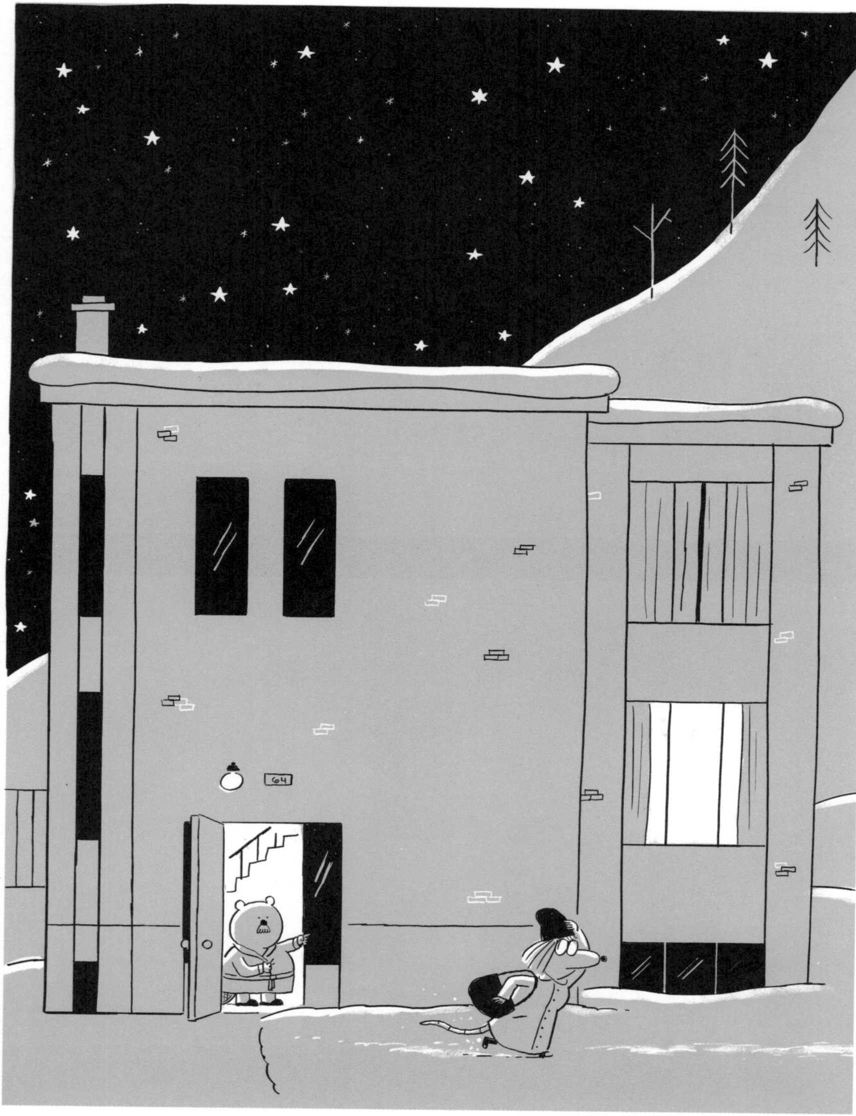
64

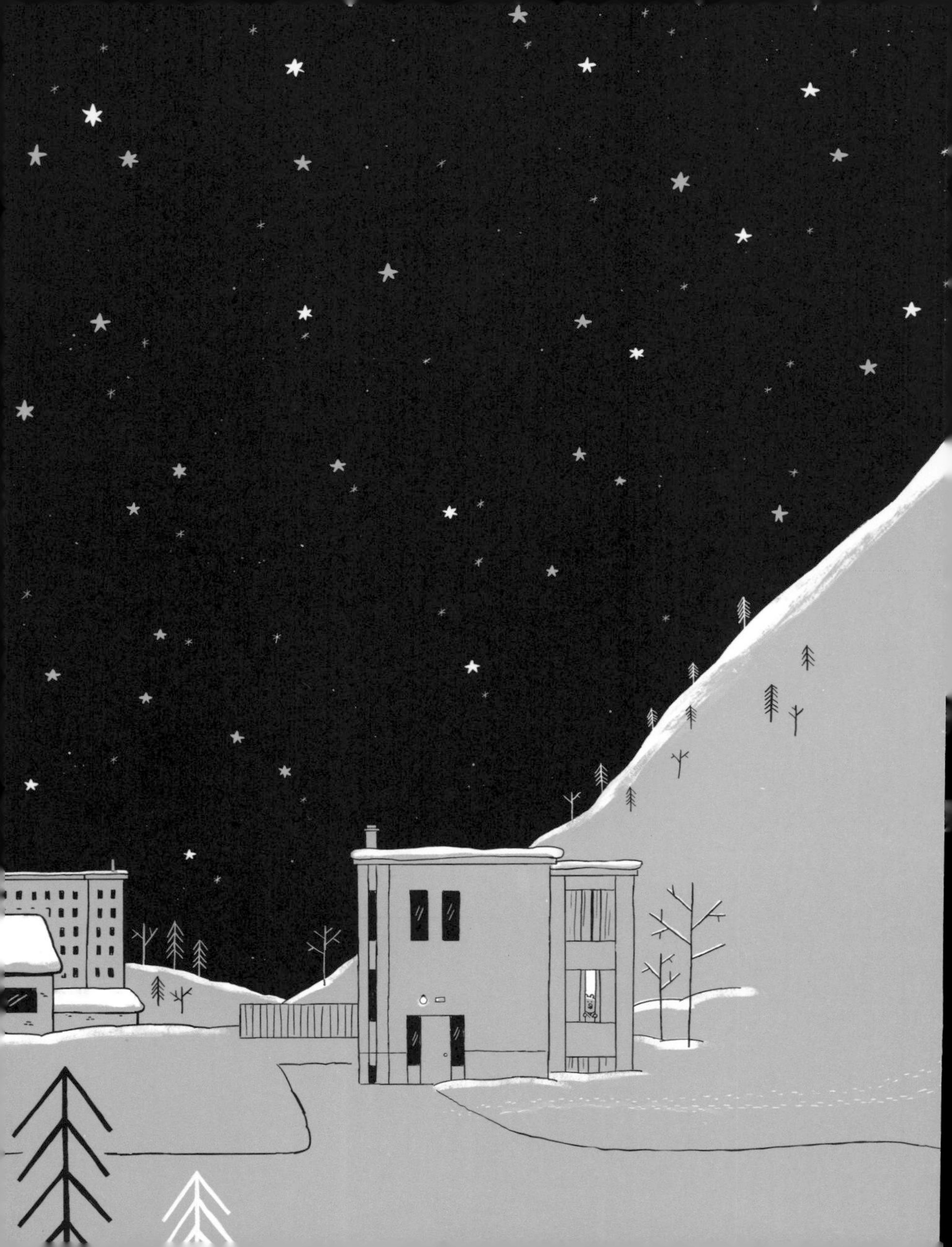

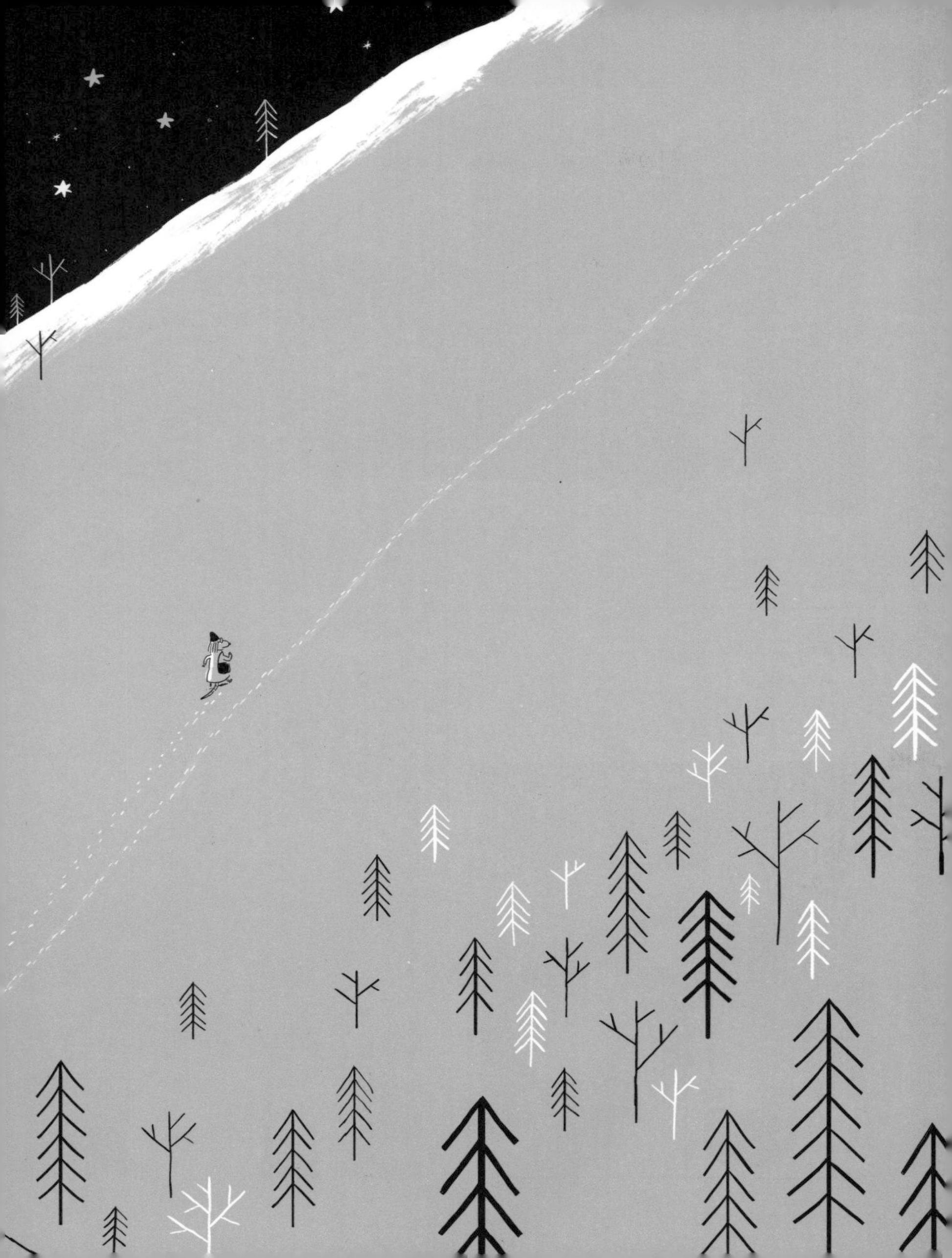

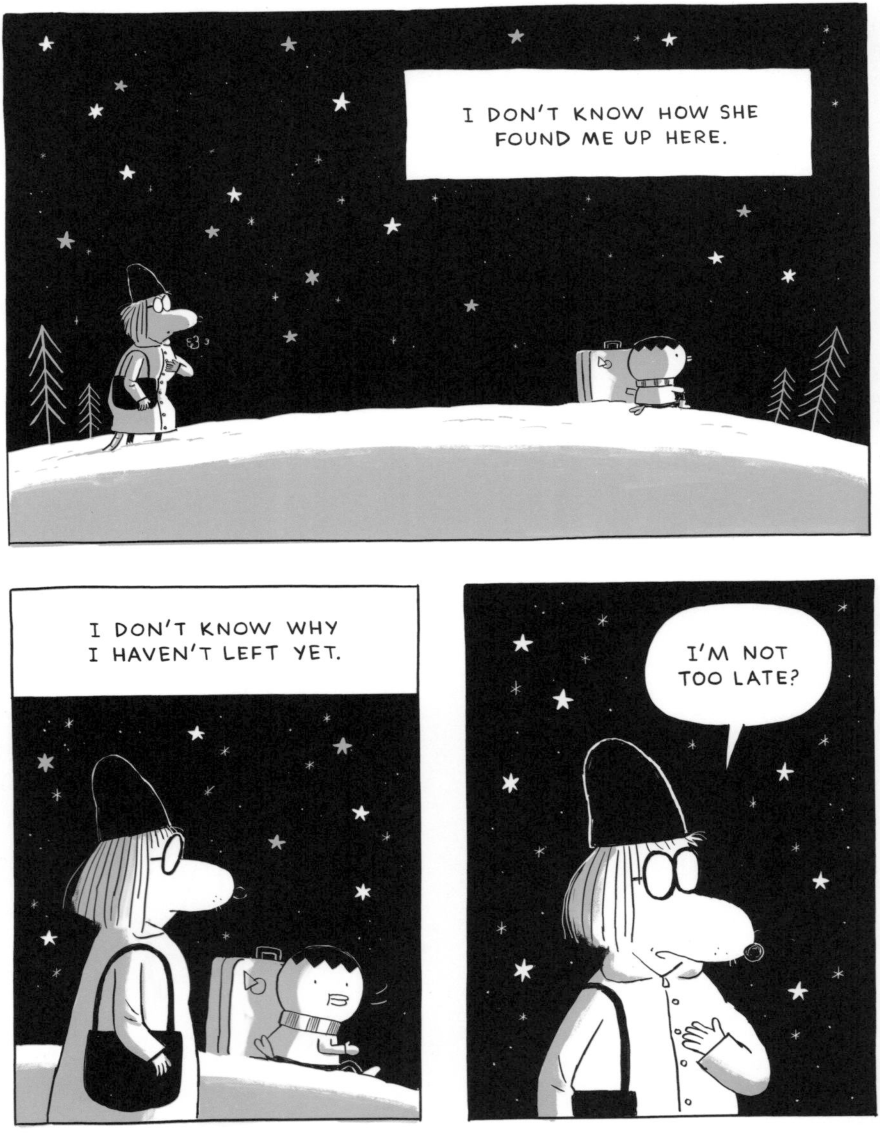
I DON'T KNOW HOW SHE FOUND ME UP HERE.
I DON'T KNOW WHY I HAVEN'T LEFT YET.
I'M NOT TOO LATE?

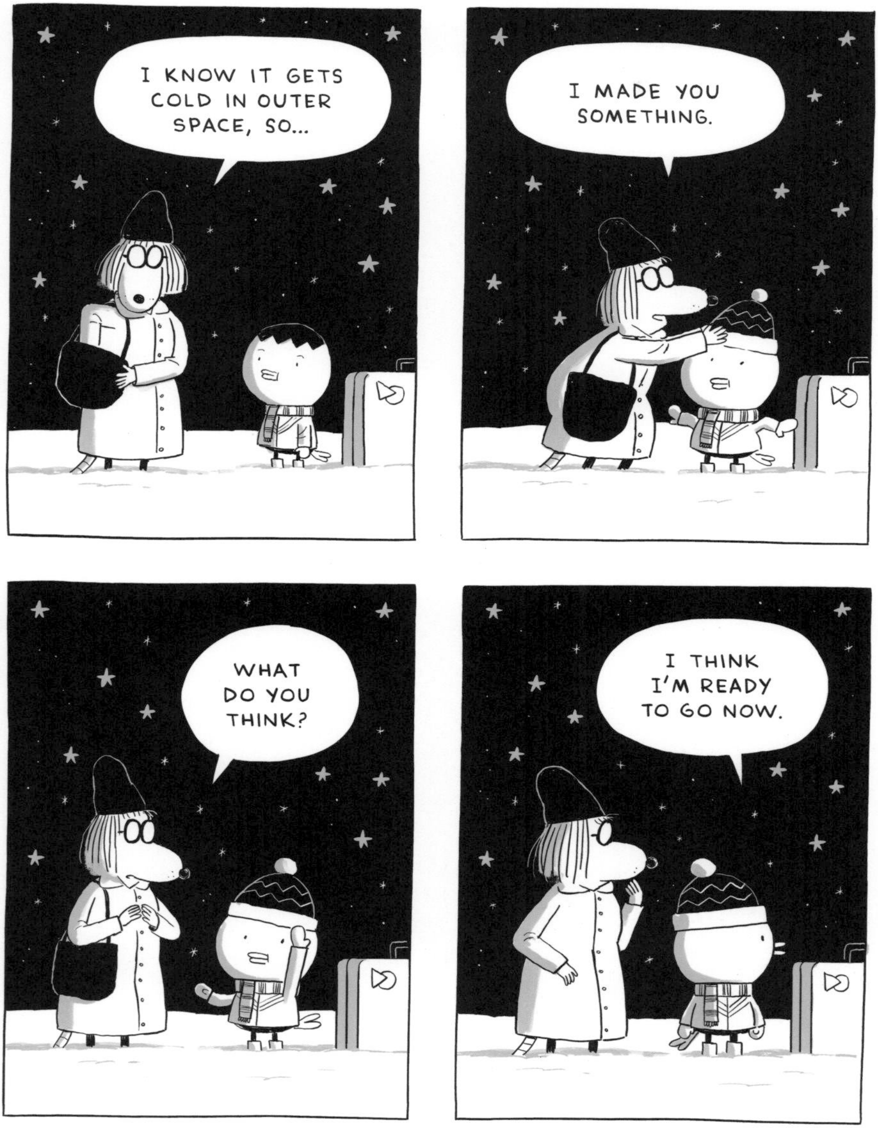
I KNOW IT GETS COLD IN OUTER SPACE, SO...
I MADE YOU SOMETHING.
WHAT DO YOU THINK?
I THINK I'M READY TO GO NOW.

"Go where?" I ask.

"Home," he says.

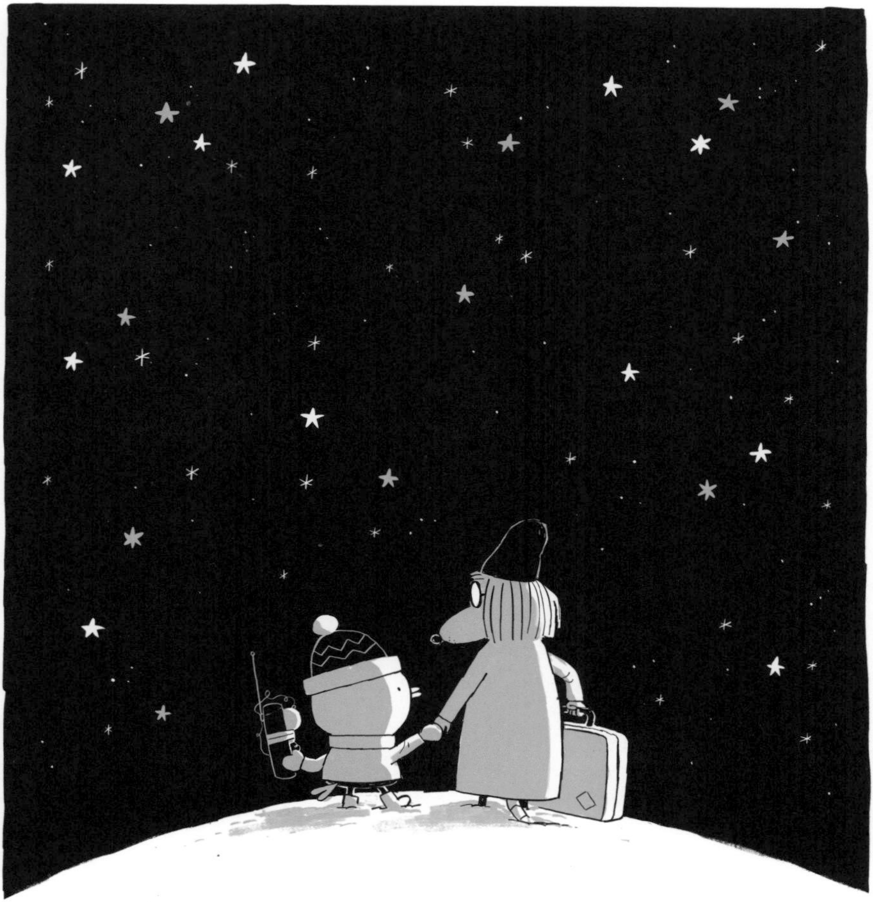

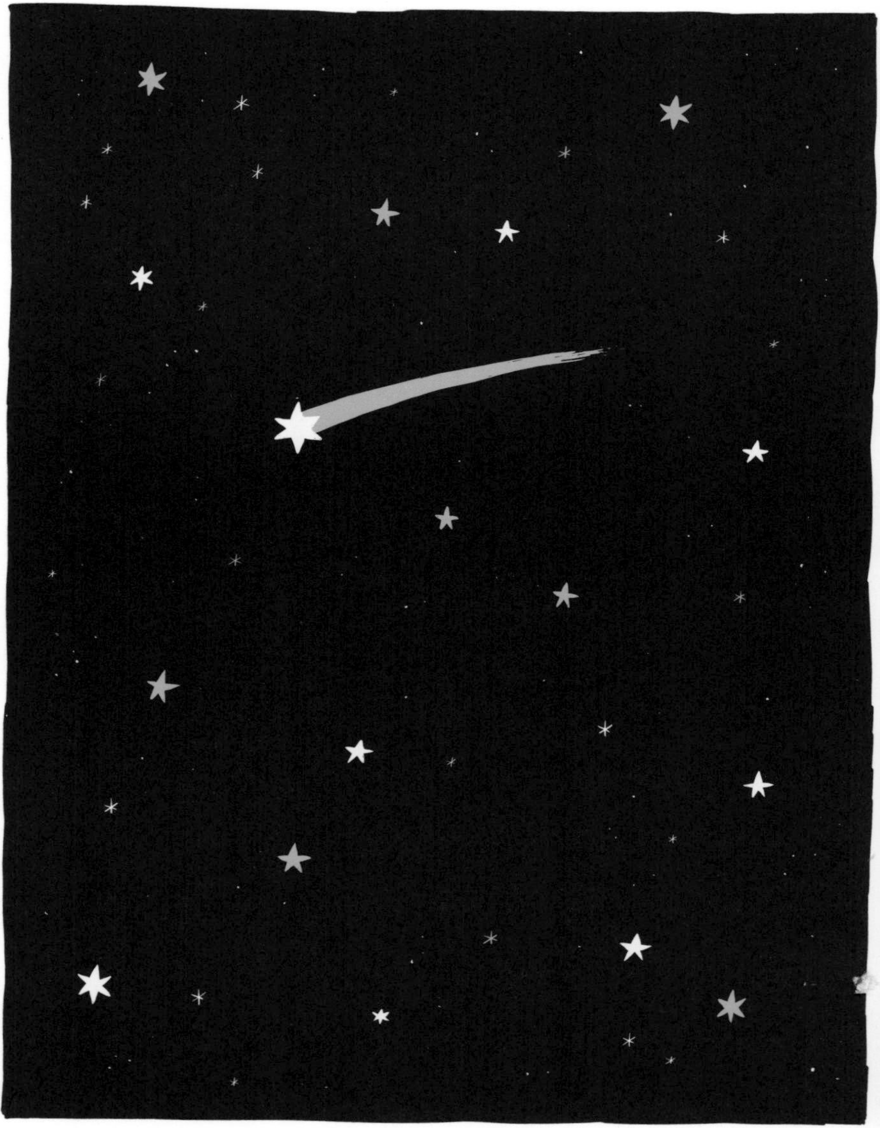